THE WORKS OF ANATOLE FRANCE
IN AN ENGLISH TRANSLATION
EDITED BY FREDERIC CHAPMAN

THE AMETHYST RING

I0636098

THE AMETHYST RING
BY ANATOLE FRANCE

A TRANSLATION BY
B. DRILLIEN

LONDON : JOHN LANE, THE BODLEY HEAD
NEW YORK : JOHN LANE COMPANY MCMXIX

THE AMETHYST RING

THE AMETHYST RING

CHAPTER I

RUE to her word, Madame Bergeret quitted the conjugal roof and betook herself to the house of her mother, the widow Pouilly.

As the time for her departure drew near, she had half a mind not to go, and with a little coaxing would have consented to forget the past and resume the old life with her husband, at the same time vaguely despising M. Bergeret as the injured party.

She was quite ready to forgive and forget, but the unbending esteem in which she was held by the circle in which she moved did not allow of such a course. Madame Dellion had made it clear to her that any such weakness on her part would be judged unfavourably; all the drawing-rooms in the place were unanimous upon that score. There was but one opinion among the tradespeople: Madame Bergeret *must* return to her mother. In this way did they uphold the proprieties and, at the same time, rid themselves of a thoughtless, common, compromising person, whose vulgarity was apparent even to the vulgar, and who was a burden on everybody about her. They made her believe there was something heroic in her conduct.

"I have the greatest admiration for you, my child," said old Madame Dutilleul from the depths of her easy chair, she who had survived four husbands, and was a truly terrible woman. People suspected her of everything, except of ever having loved, and in her old age she was honoured and respected by all.

Madame Bergeret was delighted at having inspired sympathy in Madame Dellion and admiration in Madame Dutilleul, and still she could not finally make up her mind to go, for she was of a homely disposition and accustomed to regular habits and quite content to live on in idleness and deceit. Having grasped this fact, M. Bergeret redoubled his efforts to ensure his deliverance. He stoutly upheld Marie, the servant, who kept every one in the house in a state of wretchedness and trepidation, was suspected of harbouring thieves and cut-throats in her kitchen, and only brought herself into prominence by the catastrophes she caused.

Four days before the time appointed for Madame Bergeret's departure, this girl, who was drunk as usual, upset a lighted lamp in her mistress's

room and set fire to the blue chintz bed-curtains.
Madame Bergeret was spending the day with her
friend, Madame Lacarelle. She returned and, amid
the dreadful stillness of the house, beheld on entering her room the evidences of the disaster. She
called and called in vain for her stony-hearted husband and her besotted maid, then stood gazing at
the smoke-blackened ceiling and the dismal ravages
of the fire. This commonplace accident assumed in
her eyes a mystic significance that frightened her.
But presently as the candle began to flicker she lay
down, tired out and very cold, upon her bed under
the skeleton of the charred canopy whose black
shreds fluttered like the wings of a bat. The next
morning, on waking, she wept for her blue curtains,
the souvenir and symbol of her youth ; bare-footed,
with dishevelled hair, smothered with blacks and
clad only in her nightdress, she ran desperately about
the rooms, crying and moaning. M. Bergeret took
no notice of her ; for him she had ceased to exist.

That evening, with the help of the girl Marie,
she drew her bed into the middle of the dreary
room. But now she realized that this room could
never again be a resting-place for her, and that she
must leave the home where for fifteen years she
had fulfilled the duties of daily life.

Moreover, the ingenious Bergeret, having taken
rooms for his daughter Pauline and himself in a

little house in the Place Saint-Exupère, was busy moving out and moving in.

He went backwards and forwards ceaselessly between the two houses, keeping close to the walls, and trotting along with the agility of a mouse suddenly unearthed in a heap of debris. His heart was glad within him, but he concealed his joy, for he was a prudent man.

Having been told that, at an early date, she must hand over the keys of the house to the landlord, Madame Bergeret in like manner set about despatching her furniture to her mother, who lived in a maisonnette on the ramparts of a little northern town. She made bundles of clothes and of linen, pushed the furniture about, gave orders to the men, sneezed in the dusty atmosphere, and wrote out labels addressed to " Madame Veuve Pouilly."

From her labours Madame Bergeret derived moral assistance, for it is good for mankind to work. It takes a man's mind off his own life and turns him away from dreadful self-examination; it keeps him from that which makes solitude unbearable, the contemplation of that other being, his real self. It is the sovereign remedy for moral and æsthetic obsessions. Work is also excellent, in that it panders to our vanity, hides from us our impotence, and flatters us with the hope of something good to come. We imagine that it enables us to steal a march on

Fate. Failing to realize the necessary relation between individual endeavour and the mechanism of the universe, we fondly imagine that our efforts are directed to our own advantage against the rest of the machine. Work gives us illusory determination, strength and independence, and makes us as gods in our own eyes. We appear to ourselves as so many heroes, genii, demons, demiurges, gods—yes, as God Himself. And, in fact, man has always conceived of God as a worker. Thus it was that the removal restored Madame Bergeret's natural gaiety and the joyous energy of her physical strength. She sang songs as she tied up parcels ; the rapid flow of blood in her veins made her content, and she looked forward to a happy future.

She painted in glowing colours her life in the little Flemish town where she would live with her mother and her two younger daughters. There she hoped to grow young again, to be brilliant and admired, to have attention offered her, and to find sympathy. Who could say whether, once the decree *nisi* was granted in her favour, a second and wealthy marriage were not awaiting her in her native town ? Was it not quite possible that she might marry a good-tempered, sensible man, a country gentleman, an agriculturist or a Government official, somebody quite different from M. Bergeret ?

The packing-up also afforded her peculiar satisfaction, for from it she derived some solid advantages in the way of gain. Not satisfied with the appropriation of what she had brought as her marriage portion, and a large share of the common property, she heaped into her trunks things which she ought in ordinary fairness to have left to others. In this way she packed among her underclothes a silver cup which had belonged to M. Bergeret's maternal grandmother. Again, she added to her own jewels which, be it said, were of no great value, the watch and chain of M. Bergeret's father, a professor at the University, who, having refused in 1852 to swear fidelity to the Empire, had died in 1873, poor and forgotten.

Madame Bergeret interrupted her packing only to go and pay her farewell calls, visits both sad and triumphant. Public opinion was in her favour. Men's judgments are diverse, and there is no place in the world where there is undivided and unanimous opinion on any single subject. *Tradidit mundum disputationibus eorum.* Madame Bergeret herself was the subject of polite discussion and of secret dissent. The greater number of the ladies of her acquaintance considered her irreproachable, otherwise they would not have received her at their houses. There were a few, however, who suspected that her adventure with M. Roux had not been quite blameless; some of them even went so far as to say so. One blamed her, another excused her, a third approved of her, casting all the blame upon M. Bergeret, as being a spiteful man.

That point, too, was open to doubt. Some people declared M. Bergeret to be a nice, quiet man, the only thing to dislike in him being his too subtle mind, which was at variance with public opinion.

M. de Terremondre said that M. Bergeret was a very nice sort of man ; to which Madame Dellion replied that if he were really a good man he would have stood by his wife, however wicked she was.

" There would be some merit in that," she said. " There is nothing noble in putting-up with a charming woman."

Another opinion of Madame Dellion's was : " M. Bergeret is doing his utmost to keep his wife, but she is leaving him, and quite right too ! It serves M. Bergeret right."

Thus did Madame Dellion express opinions which were inconsistent, for human thought has ever depended not upon force of reason but on violence of feeling.

Although the world is known to be uncertain in its judgment, Madame Bergeret would have gone from the town in possession of a good reputation, if on the very eve of her departure, when paying her farewell visit to Madame Lacarelle, she had not met M. Lacarelle alone in the drawing-room.

M. Gustave Lacarelle, chief clerk at the *préfecture*, had a long, thick, fair moustache, which, while the chief characteristic of his countenance, was also destined to determine his character. In his student days at the Law Schools, his comrades had discovered in him a resemblance to the ancient Gauls, as depicted in the sculpture and paintings of the later romanticists. Other more careful observers, remarking that the long strands of hair were situated under a snub nose and placid eyes, gave Lacarelle the name of "The Seal." The latter, however, did not prevail against that of "The Gaul." Lacarelle became "The Gaul" to his companions, who consequently made up their minds that he ought to be a great drinker, a great fighter, and a devil with the women, in order that he might conform in reality to the Frenchman of immemorial tradition. At the Corps dinners he was forced to drink far more than he wanted, and he could never go into a *brasserie* with his friends without being pushed up against some tray-laden waitress. When he married and returned to his native town, and, by what was a great stroke of fortune in those days, obtained a post in the Central Administration of the department from which he hailed, Gustave Lacarelle continued to be called "The Gaul" by the most important of the magistrates, lawyers, and Government officials who

frequented his house.   The ignorant mob, however, did not bestow this name upon him until
1895, in which year a statue to Eporedorix was
erected and unveiled on the Pont National.

Twenty-two years previously, under the presi-
dency of M. Thiers, it had been decided that sub-
scriptions should be invited for the erection of a
statue to the Gaulish chief Eporedorix, who, in the
year 52 B.C., led the river tribes against Cæsar, and
imperilled the small Roman garrison by cutting
down the wooden bridge built by them to ensure
communication with the rest of the Army.   The
archæologists of the little county town firmly
believed that this feat of arms had been accomplished in their town, founding their belief on a
passage in the *Commentaries* which all the learned
societies of the district quoted as a proof of the
fact that the wooden bridge cut down by Eporedorix
was situated in *their* particular town.   There is a
great deal of uncertainty with regard to Cæsar's
geography, and local patriotism is both fierce and
jealous.   The chief town of the department, three
sous-préfectures, and four smaller towns quarrelled for the glory of having slaughtered the
Romans by the hand of Eporedorix.

Competent authority decided the question in
favour of the capital town of the department.   It
was an unfortified town, which much to its sorrow

B

and anger had been forced in 1870 after one hour's
bombardment to allow the enemy to enter its walls,
walls which in the time of Louis XI had been
crumbling to pieces, and now lay concealed beneath
the ivy that had overgrown them.

The town had undergone the hardships and
privations of military occupation. It had suffered
and atoned. The project of erecting a monument
to the memory of the Gaulish chief was received
with enthusiasm by the townspeople, who were
experiencing the humiliation of defeat, and were
all the more grateful to their long-dead compatriot
for providing them with something of which they
could be proud. Resuscitated after fifteen hundred
years of oblivion, Eporedorix united all the citizens
in a bond of filial devotion. The name of the hero
roused no distrust in any of the different political
parties which were then dividing France. Oppor-
tunists, Radicals, Constitutionalists, Royalists, Or-
leanists, Bonapartists, they all gave to the scheme ;
half the cost was subscribed within the year, and
deputies of the department obtained from the
Government what was wanting to make up the
required sum.

The order for the statue of Eporedorix was given
to Mathieu Michel, David d'Angers' youngest
pupil, he whom the Master had called his Benjamin.
Mathieu Michel, who was then in his fiftieth year,

at once set to work, and attacked the clay with a generous, if somewhat cramped, hand, for the republican sculptor had done but little work during the Empire. In less than two years, however, he finished the figure, a plaster model of which was exhibited in the Salon of 1873, among many other Gaulish chiefs gathered together among the palms and begonias under the huge glass dome. Owing to the endless formalities insisted upon by the authorities, the statue was not finally completed in marble for another five years. After this, so many administrative difficulties, so many disputes arose, between the town and the Government, that it looked as though the statue of Eporedorix would never be erected upon the Pont National.

In 1895, however, the work was accomplished, and the statue, arriving from Paris, was received by the *préfet*, who solemnly handed it over to the mayor of the town. Mathieu Michel accompanied his work. He was then over seventy, and the whole town turned out to look at the old man with his lion-like head and long, flowing, white hair.

The inauguration took place on the 7th of June, when M. Dupont was Minister of Public Instruction, M. Worms-Clavelin *préfet* of the department, and M. Trumelle mayor of the town. Doubtless the enthusiasm was not what it would have been on the morrow of the invasion, when indignation was at its height, but at any rate everybody was satisfied. The speeches and also the uniforms of the officers met with applause, and when the green veil which hid Eporedorix from view was withdrawn the whole town cried as with one voice, " Lacarelle ! it is Lacarelle ! it is the image of Lacarelle ! "

This, to tell the truth, was by no means correct. Mathieu Michel, the pupil and emulator of David d'Angers, he whom the venerable master called the child of his old age, the republican sculptor and patriot, insurgent in '48, volunteer in '70, had not portrayed M. Gustave Lacarelle in this marble hero. No, indeed ! This chief, with his shy and gentle look, clasping his lance, and seeming, under his wide-winged helmet, to be meditating upon the poetry of Chateaubriand and the historic philosophy of Henri Martin, this warrior, steeped in romantic melancholy, was not, in spite of what the people cried, the true portrait of M. Lacarelle.

The *préfet's* secretary had big, prominent eyes, a short, snub nose, flabby cheeks, and a double chin. Mathieu Michel's Eporedorix gazed with deep-set orbs into the distance. His nose was Grecian, and the contour of his face pure and classical. But, like M. Lacarelle, he had a tremendous moustache, the long, curving branches of which were visible from every point of view.

Struck by this resemblance, the crowd unani-

mously bestowed upon M. Lacarelle the glorious
name of Eporedorix, and from that time the
secretary of the *préfet* found himself compelled
to personate in public the popular idea of the
Gaul, and to conform to it by word and deed
under all circumstances. Lacarelle was fairly
successful, for he had had plenty of practice since
his student days, and all that was required of him
was to be hail-fellow-well-met with everybody,
keen on the Army, and a teller of broad stories
when necessary. He was considered to be an adept
at kissing women, and so he became a great embracer.
He kissed them all and he kissed them always. It
did not matter who they were: women, young girls,
and little girls, pretty ones and plain, old and young,
he embraced them out of pure Gaulishness, and
with no evil intentions, for he was a moral man.

And that is why, coming unexpectedly upon
Madame Bergeret waiting in the drawing-room for
his wife, he immediately embraced her. Madame
Bergeret was not ignorant of M. Lacarelle's little
habit, but her vanity, which was great, confounded
her judgment, which was scanty. She thought he
kissed her because he loved her, and straightway fell
into so great an emotion that her bosom heaved
stormily, her legs gave way beneath her, and she
sank panting into the arms of M. Lacarelle. The
latter was both surprised and embarrassed, but his

amour-propre was flattered.   He placed Madame
Bergeret as comfortably as he could upon the couch,
and, bending over her, said in a voice filled with
sympathy :

" Poor lady !   So charming and so unhappy !
And so you are leaving us ?   You are going
to-morrow ? "

And he imprinted upon her brow a chaste kiss.
But Madame Bergeret, whose nerves were all un-
strung, burst into a fit of sobs and tears ; then
slowly, solemnly, and sorrowfully she returned his
kiss at the very moment that Madame Lacarelle
entered the room.

The next day the whole town sat in judgment
upon Madame Bergeret, who had remained among
them just one day too long.

CHAPTER II

HAT day the Duc de Brécé was entertaining General Cartier de Chalmot, Abbé Guitrel, and Lerond, the ex-deputy, at Brécé. They had visited the stables, the kennels, the pheasantry, and had been talking, all the time, about the Affair.

As the twilight fell, they commenced to stroll slowly along the great avenue of the park. Before them the château rose up, in the dapple grey sky, with its heavy façade laden with pediments and crowned with the high-pitched roofs of the Empire period.

" I am convinced," said M. de Brécé, " as I said before, that the fuss made over this affair is, and can only be, some abominable plot instigated by the enemies of France."

" And of religion," gently added Abbé Guitrel. " It is impossible to be a good Frenchman without being a good Christian. And it is clear that the scandal was started in the first place by free-thinkers and freemasons, by Protestants."

"And Jews," went on M. de Brécé, "Jews and Germans. What unheard-of audacity to question the decision of a court martial! For, when all is said and done, it is quite impossible for seven French officers to have made a mistake."

"No, of course, that is not to be thought of," said the Abbé Guitrel.

"Generally speaking," put in M. Lerond, "a miscarriage of justice is a most improbable thing. I would even go so far as to say an impossible thing, inasmuch as the law protects the accused in so many ways. I am speaking of civil law, and I say the same of martial law. As far as courts martial are concerned, even supposing the prisoner's interest to be less thoroughly safeguarded owing to the comparatively summary form of procedure, he finds all necessary security in the character of his judges. To my mind it is an insult to the Army, to doubt the legality of a verdict delivered by a court martial."

"You are quite correct," replied the Duke. "Besides, can anyone really believe seven French officers to be mistaken? Is such a thing conceivable, General?"

"Hardly," replied General Cartier de Chalmot. "It would take a great deal to make me believe it."

"A syndicate of treachery!" cried M. de Brécé. "The thing is unheard of!"

Conversation flagged and fell. The Duke and the General had just caught sight of some pheasants in a clearing, and, smitten simultaneously with the burning and instinctive desire to kill, mentally recorded a regret at having no guns with them.

"You have the finest coverts in the district," said the General to the Duc de Brécé.

The Duke was deep in thought.

"I don't care what anyone says," he remarked, "the Jews will never be any good to France."

The Duc de Brécé, eldest son of the late Duke—who had cut a dash among the light-horse at the Assemblée de Versailles—had entered public life after the death of the Comte de Chambord. He had never known the days of hope, the hours of ardent struggle, of monarchical enterprises as exciting as a conspiracy and as impassioned as an act of faith. He had never seen the tapestried bed offered to the Prince by noble ladies, nor the banners, the flags and the white horses which were to bring the King to his own again. By right of birth as a Brécé he took his place as deputy at the Palais-Bourbon, nourishing a secret enmity against the Comte de Paris, and a hidden wish never to see the restoration, if it were to be in favour of the younger branch of the Royal Family. With this one exception he was a loyal and faithful Royalist. He was drawn into intrigues which he did not understand, made a hopeless muddle of his votes, spent his money freely in Paris, and when the elections took place found himself defeated at Brécé by Dr. Cotard.

From that day onward he devoted his time to farming, to his family and to religion. All that remained of his hereditary domain, which in 1789 was composed of one hundred and twelve parishes, comprising one hundred and seventy " Hommages," four " Terres titrés," and eighteen manors, was about two thousand acres of land and forest around the historic castle of Brécé. In his department the Brécé coverts invested him with a lustre that he had never enjoyed at the Palais-Bourbon. The forests of Brécé and La Guerche, in which Francis I had hunted, were also celebrated in the ecclesiastical history of the district, for in these woods was situated the time-honoured chapel of Notre-Dame-des-Belles-Feuilles.

" Now mark what I tell you," repeated the Duc de Brécé, " the Jews will bring misfortune upon France. Why don't we get rid of them ? Nothing would be easier ! "

" It would be a great thing," replied the magistrate, " but not so easy as you imagine, M. le Duc. In the first place, if you wish in any way to affect the position of the Jews in this country, you must make new laws on naturalization. Now it is

always difficult to make a law which will satis-
factorily fulfil the intentions of the legislator, and
laws such as these would affect the whole of our
legal system, and would, moreover, be extremely
difficult to draft. Then, unfortunately, we could
never be certain of finding a Government ready to
propose or support them, nor a Parliament to carry
them. The Senate is no good. As history unrolls
itself before our eyes we make the discovery that the
eighteenth century is one huge error of the human
understanding, and that social as well as religious
truths are to be found in their full completeness only
in the traditions of the Middle Ages. By and by
France will find it necessary—as Russia has done
with regard to the Jews—to revert to the procedure
adopted in those feudal times which offer the best
example of the typical Christian state."

"Naturally," said the Duke, "Christian France
should belong to Frenchmen and Christians, not to
Jews and Protestants."

"Bravo!" cried the General.

"There was a younger son in our family," went
on the Duke, "called Nez-d'Argent—I don't know
why—who fought in the provinces during the reign
of Charles IX. On that tree whose leafless top you
see over there, he hanged six hundred and thirty-
six Huguenots. Well, I must confess I am proud
of being a descendant of Nez-d'Argent. I have

inherited his hatred of heretics, and I hate Jews in the same way that he hated Protestants."

" Such sentiments are most praiseworthy, M. le Duc," remarked the Abbé, " most laudable, and worthy of the great name you bear. But, if you will allow me, I will make a comment on just one point. In the Middle Ages the Jews were not considered heretics, and, properly speaking, they are not heretics. The heretic is a man who, having been baptized, and instructed in the doctrines of the faith, misrepresents or denies them. Such are, or rather were, the Arians, the Albigenses, the Novatians, the Montanists, the Priscillianists, the Waldenses, the Anabaptists, and the Calvinists, so cleverly disposed of by your illustrious ancestor, Nez-d'Argent ; not to mention many other sects who upheld doctrines contrary to the beliefs of the Church. The number of them is very great, for variety is a characteristic of error. There is no stopping on the downward path of heresy ; and schism reproduces and multiplies itself *ad infinitum*. All that one finds opposing the true Church is the dust and ashes of churches. The other day, when reading Bossuet, I came across an admirable definition of a heretic. ' A heretic,' says Bossuet, ' is one who holds an opinion of his own ; one who acts according to his own ideas and his own feelings.' Now the Jew, who has never received baptism nor been instructed in the truth, cannot rightly be called a heretic.

"And again we see that the Inquisition never chastised a Jew as such, and if a Jew was handed over to earthly justice it was because he was a blasphemer, a profane person, or a corrupter of the faithful. A better name for the Jew would be infidel, because that is the name we give to those who, being unbaptized, do not believe in the truths of the Christian religion. Again, we must not, strictly speaking, look upon the Jew as an infidel, in the same way as we should a Mohammedan or an idolater. The Jews occupy a unique and singular position in the economy of the eternal verities. Theology bestows upon them a designation conformable to their rôle in history. They were called 'witnesses' in the Middle Ages, and we must admire the force and precision of such a term. The reason why God allows them to live is that they may serve as witnesses and sureties for the words and deeds upon which our religion is founded. We must not go so far as to say that God purposely makes the Jews obstinate and blind to serve as living proofs of Christianity; but He utilizes their free and voluntary stubbornness to confirm us in our belief. It is for that reason that He allows them a place among the nations."

"But in the meanwhile," put in the Duke,

" they rob us of our money and destroy our national energy."

" And they insult the Army," said General Cartier de Chalmot. " Or rather it is insulted by the wretches in their pay."

" And that is a crime," remarked the Abbé gently. " The salvation of France depends upon the alliance of the Church and the Army."

" Well, then, M. l'Abbé, why do you defend the Jews ? " demanded the Duc de Brécé.

" Far from defending them," replied the Abbé Guitrel, " I condemn their unpardonable sin, which is to deny the divinity of Jesus Christ. On this point their obstinacy is invincible. Their own belief is rational enough, but they do not believe all that they should, and that is why they have drawn so heavy a blame upon themselves. This blame rests upon the Jews as a nation, and not as individuals, and cannot touch any who have been converted to Christianity."

" For my part," said the Duke, " converted Jews are just as odious to me, more odious even, than other Jews. It is the race I dislike."

" Allow me to say I do not believe you, M. le Duc," said the Abbé. " For that would be to sin against charity and the teaching of the Church. I am sure that, like myself, you are grateful to a certain extent to some unconverted Jews for their liberal donations towards our charities. It is impossible to deny, for instance, that families like the R—— and the F—— have, in this respect, shown an example which might well be followed by all Christian families. I will go so far as to say that Madame Worms-Clavelin, although not openly converted to Catholicism, has on several occasions given proof of truly divine inspiration. It is to the *préfet's* wife that we owe the tolerance with which in the midst of general persecution our Church schools are regarded in this department. As for Madame de Bonmont, who is a Jewess by birth, she is a true Christian indeed, and takes pattern to a certain extent by those holy widows who in centuries past gave a part of their riches to the churches and the poor."

" The Bonmonts' real name is Gutenberg," put in M. Lerond. " They are of German extraction. The grandfather amassed his riches by the manufacture of the two poisons, absinth and vermuth, and was imprisoned no less than three times for infringement and adulteration. The father, who was a manufacturer and a financier, made a scandalous fortune through speculation and monopoly. Subsequently his widow presented a golden ciborium to Monseigneur Charlot. That sort of people always makes me think of the two

attorneys who, after listening to a sermon by good
Father Maillard, said to each other at the church
door, ' Well, neighbour, have we got to disgorge ? ' ' "

" It is an extraordinary thing," said M. Lerond,
" that the Semitic question has never arisen in
England."

" That is because the English are not made the
same as we are," said the Duke. " Their blood is
not so hot as ours."

" True," said M. Lerond. " I fully appreciate
that remark ; but it may arise from the fact that
the English engage all their capital in trade, while
our hard-working population save theirs for speculation ; in other words, for the Jews. The whole
trouble arises from having to submit to the laws
and customs of the Revolution. Salvation lies in
a speedy return to the old regime."

" That's true," said the Duc de Brécé thoughtfully.

They walked along, chatting as they went.
Suddenly a char-à-banc passed them, bowling along
the road thrown open to the inhabitants of the
town by the late Duke. Filled with laughing,
noisy people, it went swiftly past them ; amongst
the countrywomen with their flower-bedecked hats,
and the farmers in blouses, sat a jovial red-bearded
fellow smoking a pipe. He was pretending to aim
at imaginary pheasants with his cane as they passed

by. It was Dr. Cotard, member for the Brécé district, member for the ancient seigniory of Brécé.

" That, at any rate, is a strange sight," said M. Lerond, brushing off the dust raised by the char-à-banc, " to see Cotard, the medical officer of health, representing this district, upon which your ancestors, M. le Duc, showered benefits and glories for eight hundred years. Only yesterday I was re-reading in M. de Terremondre's book the letter which your great-great-grandfather, the Duc de Brécé, wrote in 1787 to his steward, and which proves how kind-hearted he was. You remember the letter, do you not? "

The Duke replied that he remembered the letter in question, but could not be sure of the precise terms employed.

M. Lerond immediately began to recite by heart the principal phrases of this touching letter. " I have learned," wrote the Good Duke, " that the inhabitants of Brécé are forbidden to gather strawberries in the woods. People are evidently doing their best to make me disliked, and that would be a terrible grief to me."

" I have also found," continued M. Lerond, " some interesting details on the life of the good Duc de Brécé in M. de Terremondre's summary. The Duke spent the worst days of the Revolution

c

here on his estate without being in any way molested, for his good deeds gained him the love and respect of his old retainers. In exchange for the titles of which by a decree of the National Assembly he was deprived he received that of Commander of the National Guard of Brécé. M. de Terremondre goes on to tell us that on the 20th of September, 1792, the municipality of Brécé assembled in the courtyard of the castle, and there planted a tree to Liberty, to which was suspended this inscription, 'Hommage à la vertu!'"

"M. de Terremondre," returned the Duke, "drew his information from the archives of my family. I myself asked him to go into them, for, unfortunately, I have never had the time to do so. Duke Louis de Brécé, of whom you were speaking, surnamed 'the Good Duke,' died of grief in 1794. He was gifted with a kindness of disposition which even the Revolutionists themselves delighted to honour. Every one recognizes the fact that he distinguished himself by his loyalty to his King; that he was a good master, a good father, and a good husband. You must take no notice of the so-called revelations of a man called Mazure, who is keeper of the departmental archives. According to him the 'Good Duke's' benevolence was confined to his prettiest vassals, on whom he liked to exercise his 'droit de jambage.' As far as that goes, this particular right to which I allude is of a very problematical nature, and I have never been able to discover a trace of it among the Brécé archives, which, by the way, have been in part destroyed."

"This right," said M. Lerond, "if it ever did exist at all, was nothing more nor less than a payment in meat or wine which serfs were called upon to bring to their lord before contracting marriage. If I remember rightly, there were certain localities where this tax existed, and was paid in ready money to the value of three halfpence."

"With regard to that," went on the Duke, "I consider my ancestor entirely exonerated from the accusations brought against him by this M. Mazure, who, I am told, is a dangerous man. Unfortunately——" The Duke heaved a slight sigh, and continued in a lower and mysterious voice: "Unfortunately, the Good Duke was in the habit of reading pernicious books. Whole editions of Voltaire and Rousseau, bound in morocco and stamped with the Brécé coat of arms, have been discovered in the castle library. He fell, to a certain extent, under the detestable influence of the philosophical thought that was rampant among all classes of people towards the end of the eighteenth century, even among those in the highest society. He was possessed of a mania for writing, and was the author of certain Memoirs,

the manuscript of which is still in my possession.
Both the Duchess and M. de Terremondre have
glanced through it. It is surprising to find there
traces of the Voltairian spirit, and the Duke now
and then shows his partiality for the Encyclopæ-
dists. He used, in fact, to correspond with Diderot.
That is why I have thought it wise to withhold my
consent to the publication of these Memoirs,
in spite of the request of some of the savants of the
district, and of M. de Terremondre himself.

"The Good Duke could turn a rhyme quite
prettily, and he filled whole books with madrigals,
epigrams, and stories. That is quite excusable. A
far more serious matter, however, is that he sometimes permitted himself to jeer at the ceremonies
of our holy religion, and even at the miracles per-
formed by the intervention of Notre-Dame-des-
Belles-Feuilles. I beg, gentlemen, that you will say
nothing of all this ; it must remain strictly between
ourselves. I should be very sorry to hand over
anecdotes such as these to feed the unhealthy
curiosity of men like M. Mazure, and the malice of
the public in general. The Duc de Brécé in question
was my great-great-grandfather, and my family
pride is great. I am sure you will not blame me
for this."

"Much valuable instruction and great consola-
tions are to be derived from what you have just

related to us, Monsieur," said the Abbé. "The conclusion we arrive at is that France, which in the eighteenth century had turned away from Christianity, and was so steeped in wickedness, even to the very greatest in the land, that good men, such as your noble great-great-grandfather, pandered to the false philosophy; France, I say, punished for her crimes by a terrible revolution, is now amending her evil ways, and witnessing the return to piety of all classes of the nation, especially in the highest circles. Examples such as yours, Monsieur, are not to be ignored, and if the eighteenth century, taken altogether, appears as the century of crime, the nineteenth, judging by the attitude of the aristocracy, may, if I mistake not, be called the century of public penance."

"God grant that you are right," sighed M. Lerond. "But I dare not allow myself to hope. My profession as a man of law brings me into contact with the masses, and I invariably find them indifferent, and even hostile to religion. Let me tell you, M. l'Abbé, that my experience of the world leads me to share in the deep sorrow of the Abbé Lantaigne, and not in your optimistic view of things. Now, without going further afield, do you not see that this Christian land of Brécé has become the fief of the atheist and freemason, Dr. Cotard ?"

"And who can say," demanded the General, "whether the Duke will not unseat Dr. Cotard at the next elections? I am told that a contest is more than probable, and that a good number of electors are in favour of the château."

"My decision is unalterable," replied the Duke, "and nothing can make me change it. I shall not stand again. I have not the necessary qualifications to represent the electors of Brécé, and the electors of Brécé have not the necessary qualifications for me to wish to represent them."

This speech had been composed by his secretary, M. Lacrisse, at the time of his electoral reverse, and since then he had made a point of quoting it on every possible occasion.

Just at that moment three ladies, descending the terrace steps, came along the great drive towards them.

They were the three Brécé ladies, the mother, wife, and daughter of the present Duke. They were all tall, massive, and freckled, with smooth hair tightly plastered back, and clad in black dresses and thick boots. They were on their way to the church of Notre-Dame-des-Belles-Feuilles, situated by the side of a well half-way between the town and the château.

The General suggested that they should accompany the ladies.

"Nothing could be more delightful," said M. Lerond.

"True," assented the Abbé, "and all the more so because the sacred edifice, which has lately been restored and richly redecorated by the care of the Duke, is most delightful to see."

The Abbé Guitrel took a special interest in the chapel of Notre-Dame-des-Belles-Feuilles, of which, in archæological and pious vein, he had written a history, for the purpose of attracting pilgrims to the shrine. According to him the church dated from the reign of Clotaire II. "At this period," wrote the historian, "St. Austrégisile, full of years and good works, and exhausted by his apostolic labours, built with his own hands in this desert spot a hut, where he could pass his days in meditation, and await the approach of blessed death; he also erected an oratory, in which he placed a miraculous statue of the Blessed Virgin."

This assertion had been vigorously contested by M. Mazure in the *Phare*. The keeper of the departmental archives maintained that the worship of Mary came well after the sixth century, and that at the time in which St. Austrégisile was supposed to have lived there were no statues of the Virgin. To which the Abbé Guitrel replied in the *Semaine Religieuse* that before the birth of Jesus Christ the Druids themselves worshipped the image of

the Virgin who was to bear a son, and thus our old
earth that was to witness the remarkable spread of
the worship of Mary contained her altars and
images, prophetic in significance as the warnings of
the sibyls, to herald her appearance upon it.
Therefore, argued he, there was nothing strange in
St. Austrégisile's possessing an image of the Blessed
Virgin as early as the reign of Clotaire II. M.
Mazure had treated the arguments of the Abbé as
idle fancies, and no one, save M. Bergeret, whose
curiosity was unbounded, had read the record of
this logomachy.

" The sanctuary erected by the holy apostle,"
went on the Abbé Guitrel's pamphlet, " was rebuilt with great magnificence in the thirteenth
century. At the time of the wars of religion that
devastated the country during the sixteenth century,
the Protestants fired the chapel, without, however,
being able to destroy the statue, which by a
miracle escaped the flames. The church was rebuilt at the behest of King Louis XIV and his pious
mother, but during the Reign of Terror was totally
destroyed by the commissioners of the Convention,
who carried the miraculous statue, together with the
furniture of the chapel, into the courtyard at Brécé
and made a bonfire of the whole. Fortunately, however, one of the Virgin's feet was saved from the
flames by a good peasant-woman, who wrapped it

carefully in old rags and hid it in a cauldron, where it was discovered in 1815. This foot was included in a new statue which, thanks to the generosity of the Duke, was executed in Paris in 1852."

The Abbé Guitrel went on to enumerate the miracles accomplished from the sixth century up to the present time by the intervention of Notre-Dames-des-Belles-Feuilles, who was in particular request for the cure of diseases of the respiratory organs and the lungs. And he further affirmed that in 1871 she had turned the Germans aside from the town and miraculously healed of their wounds two soldiers quartered at the château of Brécé, which had been turned into a hospital.

They reached the bottom of a narrow valley with a stream flowing between moss-grown stones. On an irregular platform of sandstone, surrounded by dwarf oak trees, rose the oratory of Notre-Dame-des-Belles-Feuilles, newly constructed from the plans of M. Quatrebarbe, the diocesan architect, in that modern namby-pamby style which people fondly imagine to be Gothic.

"This oratory," said the Abbé Guitrel, "was burned down in 1559 by the Calvinists, and again in 1793 by the revolutionaries, and nothing remained but a mass of ruins. Like another Nehemiah, the Duc de Brécé has rebuilt the sanctuary. The Pope, this year, has granted to it numerous indulgences, no doubt with the object of quickening the worship of the Blessed Virgin in this country. Monseigneur Charlot himself celebrated the Holy Eucharist here, and since then pilgrims have flocked to the shrine. They come from all parts of the diocese, and even farther. There is no doubt that such co-operation and zeal must draw special blessings on the country. I myself had the felicity of bringing to the feet of la Vierge des Belles-Feuilles several respectable families of the Tintel-leries. And, with the permission of the Duke, I have more than once celebrated Mass at this favoured altar."

"That is true," said the Duchess. "And it is noticeable that the Abbé takes more interest in our chapel than the Curé of Brécé himself."

"Good M. Traviès!" said the Duke. "He is an excellent priest, but an inveterate sportsman, and all he thinks of is shooting. The other day, on returning from the administration of extreme unction to a dying man, he brought down three partridges."

"Now that the branches are devoid of leaves," said the Abbé, "you can see the chapel, which, in the summer, is entirely hidden by the thick foliage."

"One of the reasons which made me determine

to rebuild the chapel of Notre-Dame-des-Belles-Feuilles," said the Duke, " was that on examining the family archives, I found that the battle-cry of the Brécés was ' Brécé Notre-Dame ! ' "

" How very strange ! " remarked General Cartier de Chalmot,

" Is it not ? " replied Madame de Brécé.

Just as the ladies, followed by M. Lerond, were crossing the rustic bridge that spans the stream, a ragged girl of thirteen or fourteen, with hair of the same dirty white colour as her face, slipping from a copse on the opposite side of the hollow, ran up the steps and rushed into the oratory.

" There's Honorine," said Madame de Brécé.

" I've been wanting to see her for a long time," said M. Lerond, " and I must thank you, Madame, for being the means of satisfying my curiosity. I have heard so much about her ! "

" Yes, indeed," said General Cartier de Chalmot. " The young girl in question has been subjected to many and searching inquiries."

" M. de Goulet," put in the Abbé, " comes regularly to the sanctuary of Notre-Dame-des-Belles-Feuilles. It is his pleasure and delight to spend long hours in adoration of her whom he calls his mother."

" We are very fond of M. de Goulet," said Madame de Brécé. " What a pity it is that he should be so delicate."

" Yes, alas ! " replied the Abbé. " His strength diminishes from day to day ! "

·" He ought to take more care of himself," went on the Duchess, " and rest as much as possible."

" How can he, Madame ? " asked the Abbé. " The management of the diocese fills up every moment of his time."

As the three ladies, the General, M. Guitrel, M. Lerond, and the Duke entered the chapel, they saw Honorine, as in an ecstasy, kneeling at the foot of the altar.

With clasped hands, and uplifted head, the child knelt there motionless. Out of respect for her mysterious condition, they crossed themselves silently with holy water, letting their gaze wander from the Gothic tabernacle and fall upon the stained-glass windows, in which the Comte de Chambord appeared in the guise of St. Henry, while the faces of St. John the Baptist and St. Guy were executed from photographs of Comte Jean, who died in 1867, and the late Comte Guy, who, in 1871, was a member of the Bordeaux Assembly.

The miraculous statue was covered by a veil, and stood just over the altar. But above the holy-water stoup, painted in bright colours upon the wall was a full-length figure of Notre-Dame de Lourdes, girdled with blue.

The General looked at her with a set expression

derived from fifty years of mechanical respect, and gazed at her blue scarf as though it had been the flag of a friendly nation. He had always been looked upon as something of a mystic, and had considered a belief in the future life to be the very base and foundation-stone of military regulations. Age and ill-health were making a devotee of him. For some days past, though he did not betray it, he had been, if not worried, at any rate grieved, by the recent scandals. His simple-mindedness had taken fright at such a tumult of words and passions, and he was obsessed by vague misgivings. He sent up a voiceless prayer to Notre-Dame de Lourdes, imploring her protection for the French Army.

All of them, the women, the Duke, the lawyer, and the priest, had by this time riveted their gaze upon the worn shoes of the motionless Honorine, and these sombre, solemn, solid folk fell into an esctasy of admiration at the sight of the lithe young body, now stiff and rigid ; M. Lerond, who prided himself on being very observant, made sundry observations.

At last, however, Honorine came out of her trance. She rose to her feet, bowed to the altar, and turned round ; then, as though astonished at the sight of so many people, stood stock still and brushed away with both hands the hair that had fallen over her eyes.

"Well, my child, did you see the Blessed Virgin to-day ? " asked Madame de Brécé.

In the shrill sing-song voice of a child in the catechism class answering by rote, Honorine replied :

"Yes, Madame. The good Virgin remained for one moment, then rolled up like a piece of calico, and I didn't see her any more."

" Did she speak to you ? "

" Yes, Madame."

" What did she say ? "

" She said, 'There is much misery in your home.' "

" Is that all she said ? "

" She said, ' There will be much misery in the country over the harvests and the cattle.' "

" Did she not tell you to be good ? "

" ' Pray continually,' she said to me, and then she said like this, ' I greet you. There is much misery in your home.' "

And the words of the child rang out in the imposing silence.

" Was the Blessed Virgin very beautiful ? " again questioned Madame de Brécé.

" Yes, Madame. But one eye and one cheek were missing, because I had not prayed long enough."

" Had she a crown upon her head ? " asked M. Lerond, who, as an ex-member of the magistracy, was inquisitive and fond of asking questions.

Honorine hesitated, and then, with a cunning look, replied :

· " Her crown was on one side."

" Right or left ? " asked M. Lerond.

" Right and left," answered Honorine.

Madame de Brécé intervened :

"What do you mean, my child, that it was first on the right and then on the left ? Isn't that what you mean ? " But Honorine would not answer.

She was in the habit sometimes of indulging in obstinate silences, standing, as now, with lowered eyes, rubbing her chin on her shoulder and fidgeting. They stopped questioning her, and she slipped out and away, when the Duke began forthwith to explain her case.

Honorine Porrichet, the daughter of a small farmer who had lived all his life at Brécé and had fallen into the direst poverty, had always been a sickly child. Her intelligence had developed so slowly and tardily, that at first she was looked upon as an idiot. The Curé used to reproach her for her wild disposition and the habit she had of hiding in the woods ; he did not like her. But some enlightened priests who saw and questioned her could find in her nothing evil. She frequented churches, and would linger there lost in dreams unusual in a child of her age. Her zeal grew at the approach of her first communion. At that time she fell a victim to consumption, and the doctors gave her up. Dr. Cotard, among others, said there was no hope for her. When the new oratory of Notre-Dame-des-Belles-Feuilles was inaugurated by Monseigneur Charlot, Honorine assiduously frequented it. She fell into ecstasies when there, and saw visions. She saw the Blessed Virgin, who said to her, " I am Notre-Dame-des-Belles-Feuilles ! " One day Mary approached her, and, laying a finger upon her throat, told her she was cured.

" It was Honorine herself who came back with this remarkable story," added the Duke, " and she related it several times with the utmost simplicity. People have said that her story was never twice the same ; what is certain, however, is that any inconsistency on her part only concerned the minor details of the narrative. What is also certain is that she suddenly ceased to suffer from the disease that was killing her. The doctors who examined and sounded her immediately after the miraculous apparition found nothing wrong either with the bronchial tubes or the lungs. Dr. Cotard himself confessed that he could make nothing of the cure."

" What do you think of these facts ? " said M. Lerond to the Abbé.

" They are worthy of attention," replied the

priest, "and give rise, in all honest observers, to more than one reflexion. It would certainly be impossible to study them too assiduously. I can say no more. I should certainly never put aside such interesting and consoling facts with bold contempt like M. Lantaigne, neither should I dare, like M. de Goulet, to call them miracles. I reserve my opinion."

"In Honorine Porrichet's case," said the Duke, "we must consider both the remarkable cure, which I am right in saying was directly opposed to medical knowledge, and the visions which she declares to be vouchsafed to her. Now you are aware, M. l'Abbé, that when the girl's eyes were photographed, during one of her trances, the negatives obtained by the photographer, of whose good faith there is not the shadow of a doubt, contained the figure of the Blessed Virgin, imprinted upon the pupil of the eye. Certain persons whose evidence can be relied on swear to having seen the photographs, and to having distinguished, with the aid of a strong magnifying-glass, the statue of Notre-Dame-des-Belles-Feuilles."

"These facts are worthy of notice," repeated the Abbé, "worthy of the most careful attention. But one must be able to suspend judgment, and not rush to premature conclusions. Let us not, like the unbelievers, form hasty conclusions, prompted by

D

passion. In the matter of miracles, the Church exercises the greatest caution ; she requires proofs, indisputable proofs."

M. Lerond asked whether it were possible to obtain the photographs which portrayed the image of the Blessed Virgin in the eyes of little Honorine Porrichet, and the Duke promised to write on the subject to the photographer, whose studio, he thought, was in the Place Saint-Exupère.

"Anyhow," put in Madame de Brécé, "little Honorine is a very good, nice little girl. She must be under the special protection of Providence, for her parents, who are overcome with illness and want, have abandoned her. I have made inquiries, and understand that her conduct is good."

"That is more than can be said of all the village girls of her age," added the dowager duchess.

"That is only too true," said the Duke. "The peasant classes are growing more and more demoralized. I will tell you of some terrible instances, General, but as for little Honorine, she is innocence itself."

While the foregoing conversation was being held on the threshold of the church, Honorine had rejoined Isidore in the copses of La Guerche. He was lying on a bed of dead leaves, waiting impatiently, partly because he thought she would bring him something to eat, or some coppers, partly because he loved her, for she was his sweetheart. It was he who had seen the ladies and gentlemen from the château on their way to the church, and had immediately sought out Honorine, to give her time to reach the church before them, and to fall into a trance.

"What have they given you ? " he demanded. " Let me see."

And, as she had brought nothing, he struck her, but without hurting her very much. In return she scratched and bit him, then said :

" What's that for ? "

" Swear that they didn't give you anything ! " he said.

She swore, and, having sucked away the blood that was trickling down their thin arms, they were reconciled. Then, for the want of something better to do, they fell back upon the pleasure that each was able to bestow upon the other.

Isidore, whose mother was a widow, a bad woman given to drink, had no recognized father. He spent all his time in the woods, and nobody bothered about him. Although he was two years younger than Honorine, he was well versed in the practices of love, about the only need in his life of which he found no lack, under the trees of La Guerche, Lénonville, and Brécé. His love-making

with Honorine was only by way of killing time,
and for want of something better to do. Occasionally Honorine would be roused to a certain amount
of interest, but she could not attach much importance to such commonplace, everyday actions,
and a rabbit, a bird, or an uncommon-looking insect,
would often be enough to change the entire current
of their thoughts.

M. de Brécé returned to the château with his
guests. The cold walls of the hall bristled with the
evidences of massacre ; antlers of deer, heads of
young stags and of old veterans, which, in spite of
the taxidermist's care, were moth-eaten, and
retained in their staring glass eyes something of the
agonized sweat of a creature at bay, equivalent to
human tears.

Horns, antlers, bleached bones, severed heads,
trophies, by means of which the victims honoured
their illustrious slayers, the noblemen of France,
and Bourbons of Naples and Spain. Under the
great staircase stood a sort of amphibious chariot,
shaped like a boat, the body of which could be
removed, and was used for the purpose of crossing
rivers when hunting. It was looked upon as sacred,
because it had once been used by exiled kings.

The Abbé Guitrel carefully placed his big
cotton umbrella beneath the black visage of a

ferocious wild boar, and led the way through a
door on the left, flanked by two tortured-looking
caryatides by Ducereau, to a drawing-room, where
the three Brécé ladies, who had been the first to
return, were already sitting with their friend and
neighbour, Madame de Courtrai.

Dressed in black, owing to the interminable
series of deaths in their own and the Royal Family,
they sat there, nunlike and rustic in their extreme
simplicity, chatting of marriages and deaths, of
illnesses and their remedies.

On the painted ceiling above them, and on the
panelled walls, amid the sombre rows of portraits,
one caught an occasional glimpse of a grey-bearded
Henri IV in the embrace of a full-bosomed Minerva;
or the pale face of Louis XIII in close juxtaposition
to the heavy Flemish figures of Victory and Mercy
in loosely flowing robes ; or, again, the naked body,
brick-red in hue, of an old man, Father Time,
sparing the fleurs de lis ; and anywhere and
everywhere the dimpled legs of little boys support-
ing the Brécé coat of arms with the three golden
torches.

All the while the dowager duchess was busy
knitting black woollen scarves for the poor. Since
those far off days when she had embroidered a
counterpane for the bed at Chambord on which
the king was to sleep, she had knitted continuously,

occupying her hands, and satisfying her heart withal.

The tables and consoles were covered with photographs, in frames of all colours and sizes, some resembling easels, some of porcelain or plush, others of crystal, nickel, shagreen, carved wood or stamped leather-work. There were some, again, like gilded horse-shoes, others like palettes covered with colours and brushes, some shaped like chestnut leaves or butterflies.

In this assortment of frames were portraits of men, women, and children, relations by blood or by marriage ; of princes belonging to the house of Bourbon, of Church dignitaries, of the Comte de Chambord, and Pope Pius IX. On the right of the fire-place in the middle of an old console supported by gilded Turks, like a spiritual father, Monseigneur Charlot smiled all over his broad face at the young soldiers grouped closely around him, officers, brigadiers, and privates, wearing upon their heads, their necks, and their breasts all the martial decoration allowed by a democratic army to her cavalry. He smiled at young men dressed in cycling or polo kit ; he smiled at young girls. Ladies covered the folding tables, ladies of all ages, some of them with the decided features of men, but a few among them quite pretty.

"'Mame' de Courtrai!" cried M. de Brécé, as he

entered the room behind the General. " How are you, dear ' Mame ' ? "

He then returned to the conversation he had commenced with M. Lerond in the park, and, drawing him aside to one of the corners of the huge room, he concluded :

" For, when all's said and done, the Army is all that is left us. All that formerly made up the glory and strength of France has vanished, leaving us the Army alone. The Republican Parliament has overthrown the Government, compromised the magistracy, and corrupted public life. The Army alone rears its head above the ruins. That is why I insist that to meddle with it is nothing short of sacrilege."

He stopped. He was never in the habit of grappling with any question, and usually contented himself with generalities. The nobility of his sentiments was contested by none.

Madame de Courtrai, who until then had been lost in reflection as to the best way of preparing cooling draughts, suddenly looked up, turning her old gamekeeper's face to the Duke, and remarked :

" I do trust you have written to the proprietors of that paper which is in league with the enemies of France and the Army, saying that you intend to discontinue it. My husband sent back the number containing that article. You know the one I mean—that disgraceful article."

" My nephew writes to me," replied the Duke, " that a notice has been posted up at his club, insisting that the subscription to it shall be given up, and I hear that signatures are coming in thick and fast. Nearly all the members fall in with the suggestion, reserving the right to buy any single number."

" The Army is above all attack," said M. Lerond.

General Cartier de Chalmot at length broke the silence, in which, until then, he had been wrapped:

" I like to hear you say that. And if, like myself, you had spent the greater part of your life among soldiers, you would be agreeably surprised to note the qualities of endurance, good discipline, and good temper, which make of the French trooper a first-class implement of war. I never tire of repeating it: such units are equal to any task. With the authority of an officer whose life's career is drawing to a close, I maintain that anyone who takes the trouble to inquire into the spirit which animates the French Army will find it worthy of the highest praise. In the same way, it is a pleasure to me to testify to the persevering effort of several officers of high standing and great capacity who have devoted much time and thought to the organization of the Army, and I declare that their efforts have been crowned with brilliant success."

In a lower and more serious voice he added:

" All that now remains for me to say is, that as far as the men are concerned, quality is to be preferred to quantity, and what should be aimed at is the formation of crack corps. I feel certain that no capable officer would contradict such an assertion. My last military will and testament is contained in this formula: ' Quantity is nothing, quality is everything.' I might add that unity of command is indispensable to an army, and that a great body of men must obey one unique, sovereign, and immutable will, and one only."

He ceased speaking, his pale eyes full of tears. Confused, inexplicable feelings filled the soul of the honest, simple-minded old man, who in former days had been the most dashing captain of the Imperial Guard. His health was failing, his strength exhausted, and he felt himself lost amongst the officers of the modern school, whom he could not understand.

Madame de Courtrai, who did not care for theories, turned her fierce, masculine old face towards the General:

" Well, General, as, thank God, the Army is respected by every one, as you say it is the only force that keeps us together, why should it not also

rule us ? Why not send a colonel with his regiment
to the Palais Bourbon and the Élysée——? "

She stopped short, as she saw the clouded brow
of the General.

The Duke beckoned to M. Lerond.

" You have never seen the library, have you,
M. Lerond ? I will show it to you. You are fond
of old books, and I am sure you will be interested."

Traversing a long, bare gallery, the ceiling of
which was covered with clumsy painting, depicting
Louis XIII and Apollo destroying the enemies of
the kingdom, as represented by Furies and Hydras,
they arrived at a door through which the Duke
ushered the counsel for the defence of the
religious communities into the room where,
in 1605, Duc Guy, Grand-Marshal of France
and governor of the province, had founded the
library for the solace of his declining years and
fortunes.

It was a square room, occupying the whole of the
ground floor of the west wing, lighted on the north,
west, and south, by three uncurtained windows,
offering three charming and magnificent pictures to
the eye. Stretching away to the south was the
lawn, in the centre of which was a marble vase,
with a pair of ring-doves perching upon it. The
trees of the park were visible, bared by the winter
of their leaves, and in the purple depths of the dark

walk glimmered the white statues of the pool of
Galatea. To the west was a stretch of flat country,
a wide expanse of sky, and the setting sun, which,
like a mythological egg of light and of gold, had
broken and spread its glory over the clouds. To the
north were the ploughed red earth of the hills,
the slate roofs and distant smoke of Brécé, and the
delicate pointed steeple of the little church
standing out in the cold, clear light.

A Louis XIV table, two chairs, and a seventeenth-
century globe with a wind-rose relating to the un-
explored regions of the Pacific comprised the
only furniture of this severe-looking room, the
walls of which were lined from floor to ceiling with
bookcases, enclosed by wire gratings. Even upon
the red marble mantelpiece the grey-painted shelves
encroached, and through the mesh of gilded wire
peeped the richly decorated backs of ancient
volumes.

" The library was founded by the Marshal,"
said M. de Brécé. " His grandson, Duc Jean,
added many treasures to it during the reign of
Louis XIV, and it was he who fitted it up as you see
it to-day. It has not been much altered since."

" Have you a catalogue ? " inquired M. Lerond.

The Duke said that he had not, that M. de
Terremondre, who was a great lover of valuable
books, had warmly recommended him to have them

catalogued, but he had never yet found time to have it done.

He opened one of the cases, and M. Lerond drew out several volumes in succession, octavo, quarto, and folio, bound in marbled, stippled or tree-calf, parchment, and red and blue morocco, all bearing on their covers the coat of arms with the three torches surmounted by a ducal crown. M. Lerond was not a keen book-lover, but on opening a beautifully written manuscript on Royal Tithes, presented to the Marshal by Vauban, his astonishment and admiration knew no bounds.

The manuscript was further embellished with a frontispiece, besides several vignettes and tail-pieces.

" Are these original drawings ? " asked M. Lerond.

" Very probably," replied M. de Brécé.

" They are signed," went on M. Lerond, " and I think I can decipher the name of Sebastian Leclerc."

" Maybe," answered M. de Brécé.

These priceless shelves contained, as M. Lerond remarked, books by Tillemont on Roman and Church history, the statute book of the province, and innumerable *Fœdera* by old doctors at law ; he unearthed works on theology, on controversy, and on hagiology, long genealogical histories, old

editions of Greek and Latin classics, and some of
those enormous books, bigger than atlases, written
on the occasion of the marriage of a king or his
entry into Paris, or to celebrate his convalescence or
his victories.

"This is the oldest part of the library," said
M. de Brécé, "the Marshal's collection. Here,"
he added, opening two or three other cases, "are
the additions of Duc Jean."

"Louis XVI's minister, surnamed the 'Good
Duke' ?" asked M. Lerond.

"Just so," replied M. de Brécé.

Duc Jean's collection took up all that side of the
wall containing the mantelpiece and also the side
looking out upon the little town. M. Lerond read
out the titles stamped in gold between two bands,
that decorated the backs of the volumes: *Ency-
clopédie méthodique ; Œuvres de Montesquieu ;
Œuvres de Voltaire ; Œuvres de Rousseau, de
l'abbé Mably, de Condillac ;* and *Histoire des
Établissements Européens dans les Indes*, by Raynal.
He then glanced through the lesser poets and
romancers with the vignettes of Grécourt, Dorat,
and Saint-Lambert ; the Boccaccio illustrated by
Marillier, and the edition of La Fontaine, pub-
lished by the "Fermiers Généraux."

"The pictures are rather free," remarked the
Duke. "I have been compelled to destroy certain

works of the same period, the illustrations of which were really licentious."

M. Lerond, however, discovered, side by side with these frivolous books, a lengthy series of political and philosophical works, essays on slavery, printed accounts of the American War of Independence. He opened *Vœux d'un solitaire*, and saw that the margins were covered with notes in Duc Jean's handwriting. He read aloud:

" The author is right ; man is naturally good, and the mistaken social laws alone are responsible for his evil deeds."

" That," he added, " is what your great-great-grandfather wrote in 1790."

" How very curious !" remarked the Duke, replacing the book upon its shelf. Then, opening the cases upon the north side of the room, he said:

" These are the books collected by my grandfather, who was page to Charles X."

Here M. Lerond discovered, bound in sombre sheepskin, tan calf and black shagreen, the works of Chateaubriand, a series of " Mémoires " on the Revolution, the Histories of Anquetil, Guizot, and Augustin Thierry ; La Harpe's *Cours de littérature*, Marchangy's *Gaule poétique*, and the *Discours* of Lainé.

Close to this literature dealing with the Restoration, and the Government of July, was a shelf on which lay two or three tattered papers on Pope Pius IX and temporal power, a few dilapidated novels, a pamphlet in praise of Joan of Arc, which had been read by Monseigneur Charlot in the church of Saint-Exupère on the 8th of June, 1890, and a few religious books written for ladies of high degree. This was the contribution of the late Duke, member of the National Assembly in 1871, and of the present Duc de Brécé, to the library created by the marshal in 1605.

" I must lock up these books," said M. de Brécé. " I cannot be too careful, for my sons are growing up, and at any moment may be seized with the desire to come and examine the library for themselves. There are books among these which should never fall into the hands of any young man, nor of any self-respecting woman, no matter what her age may be."

And so, in his honest zeal for doing good, and in the happy conviction that he was imprisoning lust, doubt, impiety, and evil thoughts, he turned his key upon them ; and this sentiment, which, when analysed, had its share of simple complacency and the secret jealousy of an ignorant man, was not without its beauty and purity also.

Having thrust the bunch of keys into his pocket again, the Duke turned a satisfied countenance to M. Lerond.

"Overhead," he said, "is the King's room. The old inventories give this name to all the upper story. The room properly so-called, however, contains the bed in which Louis XIII slept, and it is still hung with the same silk embroidery. It is well worth a visit."

M. Lerond was so tired that he could hardly stand. His legs, accustomed all the year round to be tucked away under a desk, had had hard work to carry him through the walk on the slippery paths of the park, the tramp round the stables, and the stroll along the woods to the church; they felt limp and weak, and his feet were hot and painful, for the poor man, anxious to do the right thing, had, unfortunately, put on patent-leather boots. Casting an uneasy glance at the ceiling, he stammered:

"It grows late. Would it not be better to join the ladies in the drawing-room?"

M. de Brécé was only adamant with regard to the visit to the stables; as far as the remainder of his property was concerned he was reasonable enough.

"Yes, the light is going," he said. "We will see the rest another time. To the right, M. Lerond; to the right, please."

"What walls!" cried the ex-deputy, as he reached the doorway. "What tremendously thick walls!"

His thin face, the calm and cold expression of which had not altered one whit at the sight of the hunting trophies in the hall, the historic paintings in the drawing-room, the rich tapestries, the magnificent ceiling of the gallery, and the beautiful books with their tooled morocco bindings, now grew animated, interested, and full of admiration. He had at last discovered something to stir and amaze him, something which afforded him both food for thought and mental satisfaction—a wall! His legal mind, struck down in its flower at the time of the new regulations, and his heart, too soon bereaved of the joy of administering punishment, rejoiced at the sight of a wall, a deaf, dumb, sombre thing, which recalled to his eager mind thoughts of prison cells, of sentences and public prosecutions, of codes, laws, justice, and morals—a wall!

"Yes," replied the Duke, "the wall at this particular spot between the gallery and the next wing is tremendously thick. It is the outer wall of the old castle, built in 1405."

M. Lerond gazed lingeringly at the wall, measured it with his eyes, felt it with his little, crooked, yellow hands, studied, worshipped, loved, and possessed it.

"Mesdames," he said to the ladies on his return to the drawing-room, "the Duke has very kindly

E

shown me his wonderful library. On my way back I noticed the remarkable wall that separates the gallery from the wing. I don't think there is anything to equal it even at Chambord."

But neither the Brécé ladies nor Madame de Courtrai was listening; their united attention was given to another matter.

"Jean," cried the Duchess to her husband, "Jean, look at this!" And she pointed to a red leather case lying on the table near the lamp which a servant had just brought in. The case was round in shape, topped with a kind of knob like a thimble, and divided at the base in the shape of a clover leaf. A visiting card lay beside it. All around the table were heaps of tissue paper, that made one think of little white dogs tied up with pale blue ribbon.

"Do look, Jean!"

The Abbé Guitrel, who was standing near the table, opened the case with reverent hands, and displayed a golden ciborium.

"Who sent it?" asked M. de Brécé.

"Look at the card. I am horribly worried— I don't know what to do."

M. de Brécé put on his glasses, picked up the card, and read aloud:

BARONNE JULES DE BONMONT.
For Notre-Dame-des-Belles-Feuilles.

He replaced the card upon the table, took off his glasses and murmured:

"How very annoying!"

"A ciborium, a beautiful ciborium," said the Abbé.

"When I used to sing in the choir as a boy," said the General, "I always heard the Fathers call it a custodial."

"Yes, you can call it either a custodial or a ciborium," replied the Abbé. "These are the names given to the receptacles which hold the reserved Eucharist. But the custodial is formed like a cylinder and has a conical cover."

With frowning brow M. de Brécé stood wrapped in thought; then with a deep sigh he said:

"Why should Madame de Bonmont, who is a Jewess, give a ciborium to Notre-Dame-des-Belles-Feuilles? Why have these people a mania for forcing themselves into our churches?"

The Abbé Guitrel, with his fingers thrust into the sleeves of his coat, moistened his lips and said gently:

"Allow me to point out, Monsieur, that Madame Jules de Bonmont is a Catholic."

"Nonsense!" cried the Duke. "She is an Austrian Jewess, and her maiden name was Wallstein. The real name of her late husband, the Baron de Bonmont, was Gutenberg."

"Allow me, Monsieur," said the Abbé. "I do not deny that the Baronne de Bonmont is of Jewish descent. What I mean is that she has been converted and baptized, and is therefore a Christian. She is a good Christian, I might add, and gives largely to our charities, in fact, she is an example to——"

"I am acquainted with your ideas," interrupted the Duke, "and I respect them as I respect your cloth. But to me a converted Jew remains a Jew; I cannot make any distinction between the two."

"Neither can I," said Madame de Brécé.

"To a certain extent your feelings are legitimate, Madame la Duchesse," replied the Abbé. "But you cannot be unaware of the teaching of the Church, that the curse pronounced against the Jews was inspired by their crime, and not their race, and that therefore the attendant results cannot affect them if——"

"It *is* heavy," said the Duke, lifting the ciborium from its case, and holding it out.

"I am most annoyed," said the Duchess.

"It is *very* heavy!" repeated the Duke.

"And, what is more," added the Abbé, "it is a beautiful piece of work, and possesses the refined characteristics which are, so to speak, the seal and stamp of the work of Rondonneau the younger.

None but the Archbishop's goldsmith could have displayed such judgment in the selection of a model from traditional Christian art, or have reproduced the shape and decoration with such skill and fidelity. This ciborium is a work of the highest merit, and is in the style of the thirteenth century."

" The bowl and cover are in solid gold," said M. de Brécé.

" According to liturgical regulations the bowl of the ciborium must be of gold, or, at any rate, of silver, gilded inside," said the Abbé.

M. de Brécé, who was holding it upside down, remarked :

" The foot is hollow."

" That's a good thing ! " cried the Duchess.

The Abbé Guitrel looked lovingly at the work of Rondonneau the younger.

" There is no doubt about it," he said, " it is thirteenth century, and a better period could not have been selected. The thirteenth century is the golden age of this particular kind of work. At that epoch the ciborium was made in the beautiful shape of a pomegranate, which you recognize in this delicious example. The firm, strong foot is further enriched with enamels and inset with precious stones."

" Mercy upon us ! precious stones ! " cried the Duchess.

" Figures of angels and prophets are finely chased on the lozenge-shaped panels, giving the most delightful effect to the whole."

" That Bonmont was a rogue," said Madame de Courtrai suddenly. " He was a thief ; and his widow has not yet made restitution."

" You see that she is beginning to do so, however," said the Duke, pointing to the shining ciborium.

" What shall we do ? " asked the Duchess.

" We cannot return her gift," said the Duke.

" Why not ? " asked his mother.

" Well, mother, because it is impossible."

" Then we've got to keep it ? " asked the Duchess.

" Well—yes, I suppose so."

" And thank her ? "

" What else can we do ? "

" Don't you agree with me, General ? "

" It would have been fitter," said the General, " if this lady, who is a stranger to you, had refrained from making you a present. But there is no reason to respond to her civility with an insult."

Taking the ciborium in his venerable hands, the Abbé Guitrel said :

" Notre-Dame-des-Belles-Feuilles will, I feel sure, look with kindness upon this gift, presented by a pious soul to the tabernacle of her altar."

" But, hang it all," put in the Duke, " I am

Notre-Dame-des-Belles-Feuilles in this case. If Madame de Bonmont and young Bonmont want to be invited to my house—and they certainly will want to—I shall be obliged to receive them now."

CHAPTER III

IN their efforts to escape the sudden shower that had overtaken them outside the ramparts of the castle, Madame Jules de Bonmont and Madame Hortha ran along the sentry path up to the gate house, upon the debased vault of which could be seen the peacock, emblem of the extinct house of Paves. M. de Terremondre and Baron Wallstein soon caught them up, and the four of them stood still, trying to regain their breath.

" Where is the Abbé ? " asked Madame de Bonmont. " Arthur, did you leave the Abbé sheltering by the hedge ? "

Baron Wallstein told his sister that the Abbé was coming along behind them.

And soon they saw the Abbé Guitrel walking up the stone steps, damp but cheerful. He alone had managed to display a perfect dignity at the sudden alarm, and had preserved the calm suitable to his years and his corpulence ; he had, in fact, maintained a truly episcopal solemnity.

The race had deepened the roses in Madame de Bonmont's cheeks ; her full bosom rose and fell under her light blouse, as she stood drawing her skirts tightly around her plump hips. In her rich maturity, with her disordered hair, lustrous eyes, and ripe lips—a sort of Viennese Erigone—she reminded one of a golden cluster of juicy grapes.

" Are you wet, M. l'Abbé ? " she inquired, in that rather coarse voice of hers, so much less sweet than her lips.

The Abbé removed his wide-brimmed hat, the dusty pile of which was spotted with rain, looked with his little grey eyes at each member of the breathless group scared by a few drops of rain, and replied, not without a certain gentle slyness :

" I am wet, but not out of breath," adding, " It's nothing but a harmless shower, the rain has not even penetrated my coat."

" Let us go in," said Madame de Bonmont.

This was her home, this château of Montil, built in 1508 by Bernard de Paves, Grand-Master of Artillery, for Nicolette de Vaucelles, his fourth wife.

" The house of Paves flourished for nine hundred years," writes Perrin du Verdier, in the first volume of his *Trésor des généalogies*. " And the Royal Families of Europe were all connected by marriage at some time or other with the said house, more especially the kings of Spain, England, Sicily and Jerusalem, the dukes of Brittany, Alençon, Vendôme, and others, as well as the Orsini, the Colonnas and the Cornaros." And Perrin du Verdier discourses both lengthily and complacently on the celebrity of this "tant inclite maison" which gave to the Church eighteen cardinals and two popes, and to the throne of France three constables, six marshals and a king's mistress.

From the reign of Louis XII down to the Revolution the heads of the elder branch of Paves had resided at the château of Montil. Philippe VIII, prince of Paves, lord of Montil, Toche, Les Ponts, Rougeain, La Victoire, Berlogue, and other places, first Lord in Waiting to the King, was the last of that branch of the family. He died in 1795, in London, whither he had emigrated, to set up as a perruquier in a little shop in Whitecross Street. His estates, which had been totally neglected during his lifetime, were, at the time of the Directoire, sold as national property, and divided among a number of peasants who lived there, and founded a line of bourgeois. The rogues who had acquired the château in exchange for a mere handful of paper money, decided in 1813 to demolish it. However, soon after the destruction of the Galerie des Faunes, their work of demolition was interrupted and never completed. For two years the country people helped themselves, when so inclined, to the lead

roofing of the château.   In 1815 M. de Reu, an old
officer of the King's navy and a secret agent of the
Comte de Provence in Holland—it is said that he
was also an accomplice of George in the affair of the
Rue Saint-Nicaise—desirous of ending his days in
his native country, managed to extort a few hundred.
crowns from the ungrateful Prince, and purchased
the château of Montil.

There, poor and unsociable, he with his eleven
children, both legitimate and illegitimate, lived
within the walls which threatened to fall in and
bury them all beneath the ruins.   After his death,
one of his daughters, who never married, lived there,
and filled those halls of beauty and glory with
plums picked in the castle gardens, which she placed
there to dry.   In the year 1875 Mademoiselle Reu,
aged ninety-nine years and three months, was found
one winter's morning lying dead upon a torn and
rotting mattress, in the room adorned with mono-
grams, devices, and emblems in the honour of
Nicolette de Vaucelles.

At this time Baron Jules de Bonmont, son of
Nathan, son of Seligmann, son of Simon, came over
from Austria, where he had negotiated the loans
during the dark days of the Empire.   He now made
France the headquarters of his financial opera-
tions, bringing to the Republic the benefit of
his financial genius.   M. Laprat-Teulet, a member

of Parliament, who at that time represented the district of Montil, became one of the first and surest of his friends and allies. He discovered that, the era of ideas and strife having gone by, the time had come for big business deals. He bestowed upon the Baron his warmest sympathy and his extremely useful devotion, and the Baron, on his side, was always ready to commend Laprat-Teulet as a clever fellow.

It was by the advice of Laprat-Teulet that Baron Jules bought the château of Montil. It was then a dignified and beautiful ruin, well worth restoring and preserving. The task of its restoration was confided to a pupil of Viollet-le-Duc, M. Quatrebarbe, the diocesan architect. He removed all the old stone and replaced it with new. In the new building the Baron, who astonished his political friends by his taste in art, promptly installed his collection of pictures, furniture, and armoury, all of which were of enormous value.

"And thus the château of Montil," to use the words of M. de Terremondre, "was preserved to the lovers of our national art, and transformed into a marvellous museum by the care and generosity of a great seignior, who, at the same time, was a great connoisseur."

The Baron was not long permitted to enjoy the proud possession of Montil, with its towers ornamented with medallions, its tracery staircase, and the delicately carved woodwork of its interior. After reaching the zenith of his financial prosperity, he died suddenly of an attack of apoplexy, just on the eve of all the ruin and scandal that followed. He died in possession of all his wealth, leaving behind him a gay young widow, and a boy, who, with his short, squat figure, lowering brows, and already pitiless heart, closely resembled his father. Madame de Bonmont had kept Montil, of which she was very fond.

She led Madame Hortha to the spiral staircase, the interlacing stonework of which repeated interminably in its intertwinings the emblematic peacock of Bernard de Paves tied by the foot to the lute of Nicolette de Vaucelles. Then, picking up her skirts with a sudden, abrupt gesture, not without a charm of its own, she followed her. M. de Terremondre, President of the Archæological Society, and formerly a great lady-killer, came closely behind her with an eye upon the rhythmic movement of her engaging figure.

At the age of forty she had retained the wish and the capacity to please, and M. de Terremondre thoroughly appreciated this, for he was a susceptible man ; yet he did not attempt to make love to her, knowing that she herself was greatly infatuated with

Raoul Marcien, a handsome, choleric man who had fallen into disrepute.

"Let us go into the armoury," said Madame de Bonmont, pushing open the door. "It is warmed with hot-air pipes."

It was true that the armoury was so heated. Amidst the grotesque encaustic tiles of M. Quatre-barbe, designed after the manner of the old paving he had torn up, the hot-air gratings opened their bright brazen mouths.

Madame de Bonmont was careful to invite the Abbé Guitrel to a seat near one of the radiators, and to ask him if his feet were damp, and whether he would not have a glass of something hot.

Under the ribbed vault of its roof, the huge room glittered with a display of iron and steel such as not even the Armeria in Madrid could boast. One or two of the financier's brilliant business coups had resulted in a collection of armour not to be equalled by that of Spitzer himself.

Examples of the three centuries of plate armour were there in every form known to Europe. On the gigantic chimney-piece, guarded by two Brabançons in magnificent cuisses, a con-dottiere's suit of mail bestrode that of a horse, with open chamfron, horse muzzle, mane-guard, tail-guard, and poitrel. The walls were covered from floor to ceiling with dazzling suits of armour,

casques, basinets, helmets, salades, morions, skull
caps, iron hats, hauberks, coats of armour, brigan-
tines, greaves, solerets, and spurs.

From the shields, bucklers, and targes, of all
descriptions, radiated flambergs, Konigsmark
swords, partizans, gisarmes, war-scythes, two-edged
swords, Toledo rapiers, poniards, stylets, and
daggers.

All around the room stood phantom figures
clothed in polished and unpolished steel; in steel,
engraved, inlaid, chased, and damascened. Maxi-
miliennes with fluted and bowed cuirasses, puffed
and bell-shaped suits of armour, the " polichinelle "
of Henri III, and the " écrevisse " of Louis XIII.
Panoplies of war that had adorned French, Spanish,
Italian, German, and English princes; coats of
mail worn by knights, captains, sergeants, cross-
bowmen, reiters, veterans, by soldiers of fortune
from every country in Europe, by mercenaries and
Switzers.

Here was steel armour that had figured at the
Field of the Cloth of Gold; at the jousts and
tourneys of England, France, and Germany;
armour from Poitiers, Verneuil, Granson, Fornovo,
Ceresole, Pavia, Ravenna, Pultava, and Culloden;
worn by nobles or mercenaries, by knights or
caitiffs, by victor or vanquished, by friend or foe—
all collected by the Baron and displayed in this room.

After dinner, while pouring out the coffee, Madame de Bonmont offered no sugar to the Abbé, who always took it, and gave it to Baron Wallstein, who suffered from diabetes and had to be very careful in his diet. She did not do this with any malice aforethought, but her mind was full of other matters that engaged her undivided attention. Her depression, which, simple soul that she was, she was incapable of hiding, was caused by a telegram from Paris, worded with a twofold meaning; one literal and commonplace, obvious to all, referring to a delay in forwarding some plants; the other, the real and ingenious one, understood, to her unhappiness, by herself alone, indicated that her lover could not come to Montil but was in dire straits and forced to remain in Paris.

It was nothing new for Raoul Marcien to be in need of money. Since he attained his majority, fifteen years previously, he had just managed to keep himself going by a series of bold and clever *coups*. But this year, his difficulties, which had continued to increase and multiply, were positively appalling.

Madame de Bonmont was nearly always worried and depressed about him and his affairs, for she loved him truly and tenderly with all her soul and with all her body.

" Two lumps for you, M. de Terremondre ? "

Yes, she adored her Raoul, her Rara, with all the strength of her placid soul. She would have liked him to be loving and faithful, pure-minded and studious. He was not what she wished him to be, and in her grief and fear of losing him, she regularly burned candles for his benefit in the church of Saint-Antoine.

M. de Terremondre, who was by way of being a connoisseur, examined the pictures. They were all modern works of art, paintings by Daubigny, Theodore Rousseau, Jules Dupré, Chintreuil, Diaz, and Corot, and consisted of mournful-looking pools bordered by deep woods, dew-brushed meadows, village streets, forest glades bathed in the golden light of the setting sun, and willows emerging from the silver mists of morning. The prevailing tones were white, fawn, green, blue, and grey. In massive gilt frames they stood out against the crimson damask hangings that accorded ill with the gigantic Renaissance chimney-piece, with the loves of the nymphs and the metamorphoses of the gods sculptured in the stone. The pictures undoubtedly marred the effect of the wonderful old ceiling, the painted compartments of which reproduced in infinite variety the peacock of Bernard de Paves tied by the foot to the lute of Nicolette de Vaucelles.

" That's a fine Millet," said M. de Terremondre,

F

coming to a standstill before a goosegirl, whose
figure stood out, terrible in its rustic solemnity,
against a background of pale gold.

" It's a pretty picture," answered Baron Wallstein.
" I have the same thing at my house in Vienna, but
mine is a shepherd, not a goosegirl. I don't know
what my brother gave for this one." Cup in hand,
he began to stroll round the gallery. " This Jules
Dupré cost my brother-in-law 50,000 francs; this
Theodore Rousseau 60,000, and this Corot 100,000."

" I am acquainted with the views of the late
Baron in regard to pictures," replied M. de Terremondre, following the Baron round the room.
" One day he met me going down the staircase of
the Hôtel des Ventes, with a little picture under
my arm. He caught hold of my sleeve, as he
was fond of doing, and said, ' What are you carrying off there ? ' With the satisfied pride of the
complacent dabbler in art I replied, ' A Ruisdael, M.
de Bonmont, a genuine Ruisdael. It has been engraved and I happen to have a print in my port-
folio.' ' What did you give for your Ruisdael ? '
' The sale was in a dark room on the ground floor
and the dealer did not know what he was selling.
Thirty francs ! ' "

" ' What a pity ! What a pity ! ' he ejaculated,
and, seeing my surprise, gave another tug at my
sleeve. ' My dear M. de Terremondre, you ought

to have given 10,000 francs for it; if you had
paid as much as that it would have been worth
30,000 francs to you. The little picture only
cost you thirty francs and will never fetch a high
price, say twenty-five louis at the most. The
value of a thing cannot rise at a jump from thirty
francs to 30,000!' Ah!" concluded M. de
Terremondre, " the Baron was a clever man!"

" He was indeed," replied Wallstein, " and he
also liked taking a rise out of people."

The two cronies looked up, and saw, right before
their eyes, the very Baron they had been discussing,
the man who had been so clever all his life. There
he was, painted by Delaunay, amongst a lot of
costly pictures, his cunning animal-like face leering
out of a glittering frame.

Madame de Bonmont and the Abbé, seated together in the huge chimney corner before the fire,
were chatting about the weather and day-dreaming.
Madame de Bonmont was thinking how sweet life
might be, if only Rara willed it so. She loved him
so simply and so ingenuously. All the ancient and
modern moralists, all the fathers of the Church, the
doctors and theologians, the Abbé Guitrel and
Monseigneur Charlot, the Pope and the whole of
the Church Council, the archangel Michael with
his great trumpet, and Christ come again in His
glory to judge both the quick and the dead—all of

them put together would never have succeeded in making her believe that it was a sin for her to love Rara. She was thinking that she would not see him at Montil, and that perhaps, at that very moment, he was unfaithful to her. She knew he was almost as familiar with women as he was with the bailiffs; she had seen him at the races with ladies of easy virtue and uncertain age, at whom he had cast leering glances as he handed them the field-glasses or helped them on with their cloaks. The poor dear could not get rid of a whole host of tiresome people, to whom he was bound for reasons she found it impossible to understand, even when he explained them at length. She felt very unhappy and heaved a deep sigh.

The Abbé was thinking of the bishopric of Tourcoing. His rival, the Abbé Lantaigne, was done for. He was going under in the ruin of his seminary, smothered beneath bills of the butcher Lafolie. But there were many rivals in the field. A senior curate from Paris and a curé from Lyons seemed to be the Government favourites; the Nunciature as usual lay low. The Abbé Guitrel heaved a sigh.

Hearing the sigh, Madame de Bonmont, who was very kind-hearted, reproached herself for selfishly thinking of her own affairs. She made an effort to appear interested in the Abbé Guitrel's concerns, and affectionately inquired whether he would not soon be made a bishop.

" You are a candidate for Tourcoing," she said. " Would you not dislike living in so small a town ? "

The Abbé declared that the care of his flock would be sufficient to occupy him, and that, moreover, the diocese of Tourcoing was one of the oldest and most important in Northern France. " It is the see," he added, " of the blessed St. Loup, the apostle of Flanders."

" Indeed ? " remarked Madame de Bonmont.

" We must be careful," went on the Abbé, " not to confound St. Loup, the apostle of Flanders, with St. Loup, Bishop of Lyons, St. Leu or Loup, Bishop of Sens, and St. Loup, Bishop of Troyes. The latter had been married seven years to Pimentola, a sister of the Bishop of Arles, when he left her, to retire in solitude to Lerins and devote himself entirely to works of ascetic piety."

And Madame de Bonmont was thinking :

" He's been losing heavily again. In one way it is good for him, because he has been winning too frequently at the club lately, and people were getting suspicious. On the other hand it's a great nuisance. I shall have to pay up."

And Madame de Bonmont was much annoyed at having to pay Rara's debts. In the first place she never liked paying and, in the second, she disliked

lending money to Rara as much as a matter of
principle as from fear of not being loved for herself
alone.   At the same time she knew that when she
saw her Rara, gloomy and terrible, tying a wet towel
round his fevered cranium—which was beginning
to be discernible through the fast-thinning hair—
and when she heard the poor darling crying amidst
a torrent of blasphemies that the only thing for
him to do was to blow out his brains. she knew she
would have to pay.   You see Rara was a man of
honour ; in fact, he lived on honour ; since he had
left the Army his profession had been that of
witness or umpire, and, in the smartest circles,
no duel ever took place without his presence.

And to think that she would have to part with
more money.   If only he belonged entirely to her
and was loving and attentive.   As it was, he was in
a perpetual state of agitation, desperation, and fury,
and always seemed like a man laying about him in
the thick of a fight.   .

"The saint of whom I am speaking, Madame la
Baronne," went on the Abbé, "the blessed St. Loup,
or Lupus, preached the gospel in Flanders, and his
apostolic labours were often fraught with many
trials.   In his biography we find an instance which
will touch you by its naïve beauty.   One frosty
day in winter he was traversing the frozen countryside, and stopped at the house of a senator to

warm himself. The latter, who was entertaining some of his boon companions, continued to hold unseemly conversation with them in the presence of the apostle. St. Loup made an attempt to stop the conversation. ' My sons,' said he to the senator and his guests, ' are you not aware that on the day of judgment you will have to answer for every vain speech you have uttered ? ' Treating the exhortations of the holy man with contempt, however, they returned with redoubled zest to their indecent and impious talk. Shaking the dust from off his feet, the blessed saint said to them, ' I desired to warm my tired body against the bitter cold, but your sinful talk forces me, though still numb with cold, to quit your company.' "

Madame de Bonmont was sadly reflecting that lately, with teeth set and eyes flashing, Rara had been threatening the destruction of the Jews. He had always been against the Jews, and so had she for that matter. However, she preferred not to discuss the subject, and in her opinion Rara, being the lover of a Catholic lady of Jewish origin, was wanting in tact when he swore, as he invariably did, that he would like to rip open every " sheeny " in Christendom. She would have preferred more gentleness and sympathy, calmer views and more amiable desires. As for herself, her thoughts of love were mingled with innocent dreams of sweetmeats and poetry.

" The mission of the blessed St. Loup," continued the Abbé Guitrel, " bore fruit. The inhabitants of Tourcoing were baptized by him, and chose him by acclamation for their bishop. His end was accompanied by circumstances which I feel sure will impress you, Madame. One December day, in the year of our Lord 397, St. Loup, then full of years and good deeds, made his way to a tree surrounded by briars, where it was his habit to pray. Fixing two stakes into the ground, he marked out a space as long as his body, and said to the disciples he had asked to accompany him, 'When, by God's will, I end my exile in this world, it is there I desire to be laid.'

" St. Loup died on the Sunday following the day on which he had marked out his last resting-place, and it was done as he had commanded. Blandus came to inter the body of the blessed saint, whom he was afterwards to succeed as Bishop of Tourcoing."

She felt sad and full of compassion. She understood the reason for Rara's anti-Jewish frenzies, and excused them. The fact was that latterly, to re-establish his reputation among his fellows as a man of honour, Rara had warmly espoused the cause of the Army, in which he had formerly served as a cavalry officer. He had greatly tightened the bonds that united him with one great family—the Army, and had even struck a Jew whom he had overheard in a café asking for the Army List.

Madame de Bonmont loved and admired him, but she was far from happy.

Raising her head and opening her flower-like eyes she said:

"The see of the blessed St. Loup, apostle to—— Please go on, M. l'Abbé. I am very interested."

It was Madame de Bonmont's fate to seek, in hearts little fitted to give it her, the sweetness of peaceful love. The sentimental Elizabeth had always bestowed her heart upon arrant adventurers. During her husband's lifetime she had fondly loved the son of an obscure senator, young X——, famous for having appropriated to his own use a whole year's secret funds of a certain government department. Close upon this she had given her confidence to an extremely fascinating man who was one of the bright particular stars of the government press, and who suddenly disappeared from view in a tremendous financial catastrophe. These two, at any rate, had been introduced to her by the Baron himself. You cannot blame a woman if she has lovers belonging to her own set. But her newest, dearest, her one and only love,

Raoul Marcien, had not been one of the Baron's
friends. He did not belong to the world of sale
and barter. She had met him in a most select
circle of Catholic Royalist society somewhere
in the provinces. He was himself as good as a
nobleman. This time she had firmly believed
she was going to satisfy her desire for love, and
delicate, refined intimacy, that at last she had found
the chivalrous lover with noble and beautiful feelings of whom she had so long dreamed.

And now she found that he was like all the others,
alternately frozen with fear and burning with
rage, torn with anguish of mind and agitated by
the extraordinary adventures of a life devoted to
fraud and blackmail. But he was so much more
picturesque and amusing than anyone else! He
would, for instance, be summoned as witness in
some serious and delicate affair, and at the same
time be served with a judgment-summons at his
club; or again, he might one day be made Cheva-
lier of the Legion of Honour, and the same morning
be haled before the court on a charge of embezzle-
ment. Moreover, with erect carriage, and well-
waxed moustache, he defended his honour at the
point of his sword. But for some months past
he had seemed to be losing his sang-froid; he
spoke too loudly, and gesticulated too much,
in fact he compromised his case by his desire

for vengeance, for he was always complaining of
betrayal.

It was with real anxiety that Elizabeth saw
Rara's temper grow daily more unmanageable.
When she went to see him of a morning she would
find him in his shirt-sleeves, bending over his old
military trunk crammed full of writs, swearing
and blaspheming with crimson face. " Rogues !
scoundrels ! scum ! wretches ! " he would shout,
vociferating that they should hear from him to
their cost. She would snatch a kiss in the middle
of the curses, and be sent away with the usual
remark that he would blow out his brains.

No, it was not the love of which Elizabeth had
dreamed.

" You were saying, M. l'Abbé, that the blessed
St. Loup—— ? "

But the Abbé, with his head inclined at a gentle
angle and hands clasped upon his portly frame, was
fast asleep in his chair.

So Madame de Bonmont, who was as kind to
herself as she was to others, also fell asleep in her
easy chair ; fell asleep, thinking that perhaps after
all Rara would come to an end of his worries soon,
that she might only have to give him quite a little
money, and that after all she was beloved by the
handsomest of men.

" My dear, my dear," cried the much-travelled

Madame Hortha, in her trumpet-like voice, calculated to strike terror into the heart of a Turk, " are
we not to see M. Ernest to-night ? "

Standing there, with her big limbs and heavy
features, she looked like a warrior virgin left behind
and forgotten for twenty years in the wings of the
theatre at Bayreuth ; she was terrible to look upon,
clothed and girdled with jet and steel that flashed,
gleamed, and clanked as she moved, but, in spite of
it all, quite a good sort of woman, and the mother
of numerous children.

Awakened with a start by the magic blast that
blared from the bosom of the excellent Madame
Hortha, the Baronne replied that her son, who had
obtained sick leave, was to arrive that evening at
Montil, and the carriage had gone to the station to
meet him.

The Abbé Guitrel, whose slumbers, too, had been
pierced by this nocturnal flourish of trumpets,
adjusted his spectacles, and, moistening his lips,
that they might have the necessary unction,
murmured with heavenly sweetness :

" Yes, Loup—Loup."

" And so," said Madame de Bonmont, " you will
wear the mitre, you will hold the crosier, and have
a big ring on your finger."

" I do not know yet, Madame," replied M.
Guitrel.

" Yes, yes ! You will be appointed ! " She leaned forward slightly, and, in a low voice, asked : " Monsieur l'Abbé, must the Bishop's ring be of any particular design ? "

" Not exactly, Madame," replied M. Guitrel. " The Bishop wears the ring as a symbol of his spiritual union with the Church ; it is therefore fitting that the ring should suggest by its appearance thoughts of austerity and purity."

" Ah ! " said Madame de Bonmont. " What about the stone ? "

" In the Middle Ages," replied the Abbé, " the bezel was sometimes of gold like the ring, and sometimes consisted of a precious stone. It seems that the amethyst is a very suitable stone with which to adorn the pastoral ring, it gleams with a gentle lustre, and is one of the twelve stones that formed the breastplate worn by the High Priest of the Jews. In Christian symbolism it stands for modesty and humility ; Narbode, Bishop of Rennes in the eleventh century, makes it the emblem of those who give themselves to be crucified on the cross of Jesus Christ."

" Indeed ! " said Madame de Bonmont.

She had made up her mind that when M. Guitrel became Bishop of Tourcoing she would make him a present of an episcopal ring set with a large amethyst.

Madame Hortha's trumpets again rang out:

" My dear, my dear, are we not to see M. Raoul
Marcien to-night ? Are we not to have the pleasure
of seeing the dear man ? "

The cosmopolitan lady was well worthy of
admiration, in that, although acquainted with
every grade of society under the sun, she avoided
making a hopeless muddle of them all. Her brain
was a directory of all the drawing-rooms of all
the capitals of Europe, and she was not wanting
in a certain worldly judgment ; her kindness of
heart, too, was universal. If she had mentioned
Raoul Marcien, it was in all innocence. She was
innocence personified, and knew nothing of evil.
She was a good wife and a good mother, whose
home was a sleeping-car or a *wagon-lit*, yet a domesticated woman for all that. Under the corsage of
jet and steel that glittered as she moved with a
sound as of hail, she wore coarse grey cotton
stays. Even her lady's-maids never questioned
her virtue.

" My dear, my dear, of course you know that
M. Raoul Marcien has fought a duel with M. Isidore
Mayer ? "

And in a voice that made one think of inter-
national bureaux and tourist inquiry offices, she
related the story which Madame de Bonmont knew
by heart.

She told how M. Isidore Mayer, a Jew, both
well known and highly respected in the financial
world, went into a café in the Boulevard des
Capucines, sat down at a table and asked for the
Army List. Having a son in the Army, he wished to
make sure of the names of the officers in his regiment.
Just as he was about to take the book from a waiter
M. Raoul Marcien strode up, and said: "Monsieur,
I forbid you to lay a hand on that book. It is
sacred to the French Army!" "Why?" asked
M. Isidore Mayer. "Because you are of the same
religion as the traitor!"

M. Isidore Mayer shrugged his shoulders, upon
which M. Raoul Marcien struck him full in the
face. An encounter was arranged, and two shots
fired without effect.

"My dear, my dear, do you understand why he
did it? I must say I do not."

Madame de Bonmont did not reply, and her
silence was prolonged by that of M. de Terremondre and Baron Wallstein.

"I believe," said Madame de Bonmont, listening
intently to the distant sounds of horses' hoofs and
the rumble of wheels, "that Ernest is coming."

At this point a servant came in with the newspapers. M. de Terremondre took one of them and
glanced casually at it.

"Still the Affair!" he murmured. "More professors protesting ! Why will they insist on meddling with what does not concern them? It is only right that the Army should settle its own affairs, as it always has done. Moreover, it seems to me that when seven officers——"

" Of course," replied the Abbé, " when seven officers have given judgment, I will even go so far as to say that 'it is unseemly to raise any doubts as to their decision. It is highly indecorous and incongruous ! "

" Are you speaking of the Affair ?" asked Madame de Bonmont. " Well, I can assure you that Dreyfus is guilty. I have it from an authentic source."

She blushed as she spoke, for it was Raoul to whom she had referred.

Ernest entered the drawing-room, sulky and morose.

" Good evening, mother ! Good evening, M. l'Abbé ! "

He took very little notice of the others, but threw himself upon the cushions of a couch which stood just beneath the portrait of his father, whom he much resembled. He was the Baron over again, but shrunken, diminished, and sickly, the wild boar grown small, pale, and flabby. The likeness, however, was striking, and M. de Terremondre drew attention to it :

" It is surprising, M. de Bonmont, how like you are to the portrait of the late Baron, your father."

Ernest lifted his head and glanced at the picture by Delaunay.

" Ah, yes, the pater ! Clever chap, the pater. I'm all there myself, too, but pretty well played out. How are you, M. l'Abbé? You and I are good friends, aren't we ? I want to have a little talk with you presently." Then, turning to M. de Terremondre, who was still holding the newspaper: " What do they say there ? As far as we fellows are concerned, we are not allowed an opinion of any description, you bet ! Only a bourgeois is permitted the luxury of an idea, though it may be an idiotic one. Then, good Lord, the things that interest the big bugs, how should they interest us ? "

He sneered. His life in the regiment afforded him endless amusement. Although he did not appear so, he was exceedingly shrewd, prudent, and cunning ; he also knew when to hold his tongue, and took the keenest delight in the great and demoralizing power he possessed. In spite of himself, he corrupted every one that he approached, and was extremely pleased when he could swindle them in some way, as, for instance, when he succeeded in prevailing upon a poor and vain companion to present him with a meerschaum pipe. His greatest joy was to despise and hate his superiors,

G

and to see how some of the more covetous among
them would absolutely sell him their very souls,
while others, more timorous and fearful of compromising themselves by showing him any leniency,
would deny him, not a favour even, but the enjoyment of some right which they would never refuse
to the son of a peasant.

Full of craft and cunning, young Ernest de
Bonmont came and sat by the Abbé Guitrel, and
began to talk coaxingly to him :

"M. l'Abbé, you often see the Brécés, don't
you ? You know them very well ? "

"You must not imagine, my son," replied the
Abbé, "that I am an intimate friend of the Duc
de Brécé. That is not the case. The utmost
I can say is that I often have the privilege of
visiting in the family circle. On certain festival
days I say Mass in the chapel of Notre-Dame-des-
Belles-Feuilles, which, as you know, is situated in
the woods of Brécé. This, as I was just telling
your mother, is a source of consolation and thankful-
ness to me. After Mass I lunch, either at the
Presbytery, with M. le curé Traviès, or at the
château, where, I am bound to say, they treat
me with the greatest kindness. The Duke's manner
towards me is always simple and natural, and
the ladies are amiable and pleasant. They do

a great deal of good around here, and would
do still more were it not for the unjustified
prejudices, blind hatred, and bitter feelings of the
people."

" Do you happen to know what effect was produced by the utensil Mother sent to the Duchess
for the chapel of Notre-Dame-des-Belles-Feuilles?"

" What utensil do you mean? Do you refer to
the golden ciborium? I can assure you that M.
and Madame de Brécé were much touched by your
mother's simple act of homage to the miraculous
Virgin."

"So it was a good idea, wasn't it, M. l'Abbé?
Well, it was my notion. Mother isn't particularly
bright in the way of ideas, you know—oh, I'm
not reproaching her. However, let us talk
seriously. You are very fond of me, are you not,
M. l'Abbé?"

M. Guitrel took young Bonmont's hands in both
his.

" Never doubt my affection for you, my son;
it is the love of a father for his child; I might
even say that it is a maternal love as well, and
thus express more fully all that it contains both
of strength and tenderness. I have watched you
grow up, my dear Ernest, since that day on which
you made so excellent a first communion, to this
moment, in which you are accomplishing your

noble duty as a soldier in our great French Army, which, day by day, I am thankful to say, grows more Christian and more pious. And it is my firm conviction, my dearest boy, that amid the distractions, the errors even of your age, you have kept the faith. Your actions speak for themselves. I know you have always looked upon it as your duty to contribute towards our works of charity. You are my favourite child."

"Well, then, M. l'Abbé, do your child a good turn. Tell the Duc de Brécé to give me permission to wear the Brécé Hunt badge."

"The Hunt badge ? But, my son, what do I know of such matters ? I am not, like M. de Traviès, a great hunter before the Lord. I have followed St. Thomas far more than St. Hubert. The Hunt badge ? Is that not a figurative expression, a kind of metaphor to express the idea of membership of the Hunt ? Anyway, my son, what you desire is an invitation to the Brécé meets."

Young Bonmont gave a jump.

"Don't, for heaven's sake, get mixed, M. l'Abbé. That's not it—oh, not a bit of it. An invitation —I'm pretty sure to get an invitation to the de Brécé meets, in exchange for the utensil."

"Ciborium, ciborium, remember the Latin *ciborium !* I also think, my dear child, that the

Duke and Duchess will make a special point of
sending you an invitation as soon as they realize that
it will please you and your mother to accept it."

" I believe you !   As soon as they stuck to
the plate.   But you can tell them from me that
I don't care a flip for an invitation to see a
meet.   I don't want to stay and rot at some cross-
roads where there is nothing to be seen, where you
are sure to get all the mud kicked up by the horses
full in your face, and then be sworn at by a hunts-
man for obstructing the way.   No, I am not particularly keen on such amusements.   The Brécés
can keep their invitation ! "

" In that case, my son, I do not understand
your idea."

" And yet my idea is clear enough, M. l'Abbé.
I do not intend the Brécés to laugh up their sleeve
at me, that's what I'm driving at."

" Pray explain yourself ! "

" Well, M. l'Abbé, just imagine being planted
down on the Carrefour du Roi, together with the
village doctor, the wife of the Chief of Police, and
M. Irvoy's head clerk ! No, such a situation is not
to be thought of for one moment.   But if I wear
the Hunt badge, I can follow the hounds, and,
although I may look a bit off colour sometimes,
I'll soon show them whether I can ride or not.
Now *you* can get me what I want, M. l'Abbé;

the Brécés will not refuse you anything. All you have to do is to ask it in the name of Notre-Dame-des-Belles-Feuilles."

"I beg of you, my child, not to bring Notre-Dame-des-Belles-Feuilles into such a matter, which cannot interest her in the very slightest. The miraculous Virgin of Brécé has enough to do in answering the prayers of widows and orphans, not to mention those of our brave soldiers in Madagascar. But, my dear Ernest, is there really so much to be gained by the possession of this badge? Is it then such a precious talisman? No doubt strange privileges are attached to its possession. Tell me all about them. I am far from despising the noble and ancient art of hunting, for I belong to the clergy of an eminently sporting diocese, and would be glad of any information on the subject."

"You do amuse me, M. l'Abbé, and I know you must be joking. You know as well as I do what is understood by the Hunt badge: it is the right to wear the colours of any particular hunt. I am going to speak frankly to you; I am candid, because I can afford to be so. I want to be made a member of the Brécé Hunt, because it is the correct thing, and I like to be in the swim. I want it because I am a snob and a vain man. I also want it because it would amuse me to dine with the Brécés on St. Hubert's Day. The Brécé

badge would be just about my mark. I want
it very badly, and I'm not going to disguise the
fact. I have no false shame—no shame of any
kind, for the matter of that. Listen to me, M.
l'Abbé, I have something of great importance to
say to you. You must understand that in broaching
the subject to the Duc de Brécé, you will only be
claiming what is my due ; you understand—
my due ! I have property round here ; I do not
shoot the deer ; I let people hunt and kill on my
estates, all of which deserves both consideration
and gratitude. M. de Brécé is really under obligations to his kind little neighbour Ernest."

The Abbé said nothing. It was evident that he
did not like the idea, and was prepared to refuse
to do what was asked of him. Young Bonmont
went on :

" I need hardly say, M. l'Abbé, that, in case the
Brécés demand a price in return for the privilege,
I should not stick at such a trifle."

M. l'Abbé Guitrel made a movement of protest.

" Banish that supposition, my son ! It ill
accords with the character of the Duc de Brécé."

" That may be, M. l'Abbé. Whether it be given
or sold, depends upon the owner's ideas and the
state of his banking account. Some packs cost the
master 80,000 francs a year ; others bring him in
as much as 30,000 francs a year. In saying this I

am not in any way blaming the man who expects people to pay for their privileges. Personally, I should prefer to do so, indeed, I consider it only fair. Then there are districts where hunting costs so much, that the master, even if he is a rich man, cannot keep things going alone. Just suppose for instance, M. l'Abbé, that you kept a pack in the neighbourhood of Paris. Can you see yourself meeting all expenses and finding your purse sufficient to pay the heavy claims entailed ? But I think I have heard that the Brécé badge is not to be bought with money. The Duke hasn't the gumption to make a profit out of his pack. Well, M. l'Abbé, you will get it for me, gratis and for nothing ! It will all be so much to the good."

Before replying, the Abbé reflected long and deeply, and this display of prudence worried young Bonmont not a little. At last, however, the Abbé opened his lips :

" My son, I have said so once, and will say it again. I have a great affection for you, and should like both to please and to aid you. I would welcome any opportunity of doing you a service. But I really have not the necessary qualifications to solicit on your behalf the worldly distinction to which you refer. Just think for a moment. Suppose that, after hearing my request, M. de Brécé should refuse or make some difficulty about granting it ? I should be powerless to bring any pressure to bear upon him. What chance would a humble professor of elocution at the Grand Séminaire have of overcoming resistance, removing difficulty, and obtaining consent, so to speak, by main force ? I have nothing with which to convince and hold parley with the great ones of the earth. I cannot, must not, even in so paltry a matter as this, undertake anything without being assured of its success."

Young Bonmont looked at the Abbé with surprise mingled with admiration, and said :

"I understand, M. l'Abbé. You cannot manage it for the time being. But when you are made a bishop you will carry off the badge with the same ease as a man at a fair carries off the ring, when tilting upon the wooden horses of the roundabouts. Of course you will ! "

"It is quite possible," returned M. Guitrel, with the greatest gravity, " that if a bishop were to ask for the Hunt badge for you, the Duke would not refuse him."

CHAPTER IV

THAT evening M. Bergeret, having done a hard day's work, was feeling tired. He was taking his customary stroll in the town, accompanied by M. Goubin, his favourite disciple since the treachery of M. Roux, and as he ruminated over the work he had accomplished he fell to wondering, like so many others before him, what profit a man hath of all his labours. M. Goubin asked:

"Master, do you think that Paul Louis Courrier would be a good subject to choose for an essay?"

M. Bergeret made no reply. He was just then passing the shop of Madame Fusellier, the stationer, and, stopping in front of the window in which sundry drawing models were displayed, he looked with interest at the Farnese Hercules who was showing off his muscles amid these examples of scholastic art.

"I feel kindly disposed towards him," remarked M. Bergeret.

" Towards whom ? " asked M. Goubin, wiping his glasses.

" Hercules," replied M. Bergeret. " He was a good man. He himself said : ' My life is laborious and tends to a high ideal.' He toiled much upon this earth ere he received the reward of death, which, in truth, is the only guerdon of life. He had no time to give to meditation, and prolonged thought never marred the simplicity of his soul. But when evening came a feeling of melancholy would steal over him, and, in default of an enquiring mind, his great heart would reveal to him the vanity of effort, and the necessity which compels all men, even the best, to do evil even when they do good. This man of might was extraordinarily gentle. Like the rest of us when we commit ourselves to action, he found that he destroyed indiscriminately both the innocent and the guilty, the meek and the violent, and, when he mused over all this, it doubtless caused him more than one regret. Perhaps he even felt compassion for the unhappy monsters he had destroyed for the benefit of mankind : the poor Cretan bull, the poor Lernæan hydra, or the beautiful lion who, when he died, provided him with such an excellently warm cloak. More than once, when the day was over and his work done, his club must have weighed heavily upon him." M. Bergeret raised aloft his umbrella with an effort as though it had been a heavy weapon. Then he continued his discourse. " He was strong, yet weak. We love him because he is like ourselves."

" Hercules ? " asked M. Goubin.

" Yes," replied M. Bergeret. " Like ourselves, he was born unhappy, the child of a god and a woman. From this mixed origin he derived the sadness of a thoughtful spirit and the cravings of a ravening body. All his life long he was subject to the caprices of a whimsical king. Are not we too the children of Zeus and the hapless Alcmena, and the slaves of Eurystheus ? I am at the mercy of the Minister of Public Instruction, who may take it into his head at any moment to ship me off to Algiers, just as Hercules was sent to the land of the Nasamones."

" You are not leaving us, dear Master ? " asked M. Goubin anxiously.

" See how sad he is ! " went on M. Bergeret. " How wearily he leans upon his club, letting his arm hang limply at his side ! His head is bowed, he is thinking of his heavy labours. The Farnese Hercules was certainly conceived after the statue by Lysippus, who was a blacksmith's apprentice before becoming a sculptor, and it is undoubtedly that sturdy sculptor of a sturdy hero who fixed the type of Hercules."

Having wiped his glasses once again with his

handkerchief, M. Goubin tried to catch a glimpse of the principal points mentioned by the master, and while he was thus engaged Madame Fusellier, the proprietress of the shop, on hearing the clock strike nine, extinguished the gas under the disciple's peering eyes. The poor man had no idea why he could see nothing, for he was so short-sighted as to be an utter stranger to that imaginary world in which most men have their being.

And, as M. Bergeret continued to walk and talk, he followed the sound of his voice, for he trusted only to what he heard others say to guide him along those pathways of the earth whereon his youthful prudence told him he might venture.

" His strength," continued the Professor, " was the cause of his weakness. He was under the yoke of his own strength, subject to the exigencies of his nature, which compelled him to devour whole sheep, drink great jars of dark wine, and to do foolish deeds for women of little worth. The hero whose club brought peace and happiness and justice to the world, the son of the great god Zeus, would seek sleep anywhere like a mere tramp, or tarry for weeks and weeks with a wench whose lover he was. And this was the cause of his melancholy. With his simple soul, his submissiveness, his love of justice, and his mighty muscles, it was to be feared that he could be nothing more than an excellent

soldier or a glorified gendarme. But his very weak-
nesses, his errors, his unhappy experiences broadened
his soul, opened out his vision upon the manifold
diversity of life and mellowed with gentleness his
terrible capacity for good works."

"Dear Master," said M. Goubin, "do you not
think that Hercules is the sun, that his twelve
labours are the signs of the zodiac, and that Dejanira's
fiery robe represents the flaming clouds of the setting
sun ?"

"That is possible," replied M. Bergeret, "but I
do not wish to believe it. It pleases me to have the
same idea of Hercules that a barber of Thebes or a
herb-vendor of Eleusis would have had in the time
of the Median wars. I think this idea from the
point of view of force, fullness and vivacity is worth
all your systems of comparative mythology put
together. Hercules was a kind-hearted man. When
he went to seek the steeds of Diomedes he crossed
through Pheræ and stayed his steps before the
palace of Admetus. He called for food and drink,
and spoke very roughly to the servants, who had
never set eyes on such an uncouth guest. He
crowned himself with myrtles, and drank enormous
quantities of wine, and, being very drunk, and not
at all proud, he tried to force the cup-bearer to
drink with him ; but the latter, very shocked at
such manners, replied severely that it was no time

for eating and drinking, when the good Queen Alcestis had just been borne to the grave. She had consecrated herself to Thanatos in place of her husband Admetus. It was, therefore, not an ordinary death, but a kind of spell which had been cast over her.

"Good Hercules immediately recovered from his drunkenness, and asked whither they had taken Alcestis. Beyond the suburb on the way to Larissa she lay in a tomb of polished marble. Thither hastened Hercules, and when Thanatos, robed in black, came to taste of the offering of cakes dipped in blood, the hero, who was lying in ambush behind the funeral pile, threw himself upon the King of Darkness, held him prisoner in the circle of his arms, and forced him, all bruised and broken, to give up Alcestis, who, veiled and silent, returned with him to the palace of Admetus. This time he would accept of no refreshment, he was in haste, for he had barely time to fetch the steeds of Diomedes.

"That was a wonderful adventure, but I think I prefer the tale about the Cercopes. Do you know the story of the two brothers, M. Goubin? One was called Andolous and the other Atlantos, and they had faces like monkeys. Their name leads me to believe that they were also possessed of tails like the smaller species of the monkey tribe.

They were very cunning thieves, and robbed the orchards, and their mother was continually warning them to beware of the hero, Melampyges. This, you know, was the name familiarly given to Hercules, whose skin was not white. The two rash little creatures disdained their mother's wise counsels, and one day, having surprised the 'Melampyges' asleep on the mossy banks of a stream, they crept up to him to try and steal his club and lionskin. But the hero, waking suddenly, seized them, tied them by the feet to the branch of a tree, and slinging them over his shoulder went upon his way. The Cercopes were doubtless very uncomfortable, both in mind and body, but as the latter was extremely supple and the former happy-go-lucky, they were amused and interested in everything they could see, and what they chiefly saw was the reason for the hero's nickname of mélampyge. Atlantos pointed this out to his brother Andolous, who replied that their captor was indeed the hero of whom their mother had spoken. And as they hung like squirrels from a hunter's spear they whispered, 'Melampyges! Melampyges!' with a mocking laugh like the cry of the forest lapwing.

Hercules was a very irritable man, and did not like being made fun of, but he was not over proud, and never imagined that the whole of his body was as white as that of poor little Hylas. The name that had been bestowed upon him appeared to him an honourable one, and quite worthy of a strong man who journeyed about accomplishing great labours. He was a simple soul and easily moved to laughter. The remarks of the two Cercopes struck him as so funny that he stopped short, and, placing his game upon the ground, sat down by the wayside and began to shout with laughter. For a long time he remained there filling the valley with the sounds of his mirth. The setting sun spread his crimson rays over the clouds and gleamed on the mountain tops, and still the hero's laughter rang out from beneath the dark pines and tufted larches. At last, however, he rose, untied the two little monkey-men, and, having admonished them, let them go, while in the falling darkness he continued his rough journey across the mountains. You see he was a kind-hearted man ! "

"Dear Master," said M. Goubin, "allow me to ask you a question. Do you consider Paul Louis Courrier a good subject for my essay? Because as soon as I have got my degree——"

H

CHAPTER V

S they were discussing the Affair at Paillot's library, in a corner devoted to old books, M. Bergeret, who was of a speculative turn of mind, gave expression to ideas upon the subject that were not in accord with popular sentiment.

"This hearing of cases in camera is a detestable practice," he said.

And as M. de Terremondre offered in defence reasons of State, he replied:

"We have no State. We have administrations. What we call reasons of State are simply the reasons of government departments. We are told that such reasons are sacred; as a matter of fact, they afford the department the opportunity to hide its errors, and at the same time to aggravate their consequences."

"I am a republican, a Jacobin, a terrorist—and a patriot," remarked M. Mazure solemnly. "I am quite willing to send the generals to the guillotine, but I allow no one to dispute the decisions of military justice."

" And you are right," replied M. de Terremondre, " for if any justice is worthy of respect, it is that above all others.   And, knowing the army as I do, I can assure you that there are no judges so indulgent or so merciful as military judges."

" I am very glad to hear you say so," replied M. Bergeret.   " But as the army is a department just the same as agriculture, finance or public instruction, one cannot conceive of there being such a thing as military courts, when there are neither agricultural, financial, nor university courts. Any peculiar form of justice is directly opposed to the fundamental principles of modern law.   The military provostships will appear as old-fashioned and barbarous to our descendants as seigniorial and ecclesiastical courts appear to us to-day."

" You are joking ! " said M. de Terremondre.

" That is what has been said of every prophet," replied M. Bergeret.

" But if you attack the courts martial," cried M. de Terremondre, " it means the end of the Army, and therefore the end of the country."

M. Bergeret's reply was as follows :

" When the priests and seigniors were deprived of the right of hanging their serfs, people thought it meant the end of all law and order.   Soon, however, a new order of government sprang up, better than the old one.   What I say is this : in times of peace let the soldier be judged by a civil court. Do you imagine that since the time of Charles VII, or even since Napoleon, the Army has not survived more drastic innovations than that ? "

" I am an old Jacobin," repeated M. Mazure. " I am in favour of courts martial, and would have the heads of the Army subject to the authority of a committee of public safety. There is nothing more calculated to keep them up to the mark."

" That's another matter altogether," said M. de Terremondre. " I return to our original subject and ask M. Bergeret whether he honestly believes it possible that *seven* officers could make a mistake?"

" Fourteen ! " cried M. Mazure.

" Fourteen," repeated M. de Terremondre.

" I do believe it possible," said M. Bergeret.

" Fourteen French officers ! " ejaculated M. de Terremondre.

" Oh, well," said M. Bergeret, " they might have been Swiss, Belgian, Spanish, German, or Dutch, and have made just as bad a blunder."

" Impossible ! " cried M. de Terremondre.

The librarian Paillot shook his head, thereby meaning to express the fact that he also considered it impossible. And his clerk, Léon, looked at M. Bergeret with indignant surprise.

" I do not know whether you will ever be enlightened," went on M. Bergeret sweetly. " I do
not think so, although all things are possible, even
the triumph of truth."

" You mean the Revision," said M. de Terremondre. " That, never ! You will never succeed
in getting the Revision ; I have been told as much
by three Ministers and twenty deputies."

" The poet Bouchor," replied M. Bergeret,
" teaches us that it is better to endure the horrors
of war than to commit an unjust action. But such
an alternative does not confront you, gentlemen,
and you are being scared with lies."

Just as M. Bergeret was saying this a great noise
was heard in the square outside. A band of little
boys was marching past and shouting, "*A bas Zola !
Mort aux juifs !* " They were on their way to
break the windows of Meyer, the bootmaker, who
was supposed to be a Jew, and the townsmen in-
dulgently watched them go by.

" Fine little chaps ! " cried M. de Terremondre,
when the demonstrators had filed by.

M. Bergeret, with his nose buried in a ponderous
volume, slowly remarked :

" The cause of liberty had only the very smallest
minority of educated people upon her side. The
clergy almost to a man, the generals and the ignorant
and fanatical mob clamoured for a master."

" What is that you are saying ? " asked M. Mazure excitedly.

" Nothing," replied M. Bergeret. " I am reading a chapter of Spanish history which describes the manners and customs of the people at the time of the restoration of Ferdinand VII."

The bootmaker, Meyer, was half killed, nevertheless. He did not complain, for fear of being killed outright, and also because the justice of the people, together with that of the Army, filled him with mute admiration.

CHAPTER VI

BERGERET was not unhappy, for he rejoiced in that true independence which comes from within, and his soul was unfettered. Since the departure of his wife he was also enjoying the sweets of solitude, while awaiting the arrival of his daughter Pauline, who was shortly expected from Arcachon with his sister, Mademoiselle Bergeret.

He looked forward to a happy life with his daughter, who resembled him in certain turns of mind and speech, so that it flattered his vanity when people praised her.

He was pleased at the idea of seeing his sister Zoe, an old maid, who, having never had any pretensions to good looks, had not lost her natural frankness of disposition, to which was added a secret delight in making herself unpleasant, but who lacked neither wit nor kindliness.

For the time being, however, M. Bergeret was busy settling down in his new quarters. He hung his views of Naples and Vesuvius, legacies both, on the walls of his study. Now of all the delights permitted to a respectable man, there is perhaps none which procures him such tranquil enjoyment as that of knocking nails into a wall. The keenest pleasure of that experienced voluptuary, Comte de Caylus, was unpacking cases of Etruscan pottery. Thus M. Bergeret proceeded to hang up on his wall an old water-colour representing Vesuvius, adorned with an aigrette of flame and smoke, standing out against the dark blue sky of midnight. This picture reminded him of the days of his wondering and enchanted childhood.

He was not sad, neither was he glad. He had money worries, he knew the unloveliness of poverty. " Money makes the man," as Pindar says (*Isth*. II).

He did not get on with his colleagues or his pupils. He did not get on with the townspeople ; incapable as he was of comprehending either their thoughts or their feelings, he had been obliged to withdraw from human fellowship, and his peculiar way of thinking had deprived him of the enjoyment of that genial feeling of comradeship which even high walls and closed doors cannot exclude.

The mere fact that he was a thinker made him a strange and disturbing element suspected by all. He was even a source of worry to Paillot, the book-

seller, and his asylum and refuge, the corner where
the old books were kept, was no longer to be counted
on.   In spite of all this he was not unhappy.   He
set about arranging his books on the deal shelves put
up by the carpenter, and took pleasure in handling
these little memorials of his humble contemplative
life.   He worked with zeal at his task of getting
things straight, and when he tired of hanging
pictures or arranging furniture, he buried himself
deep in some book, with a lurking feeling, however, that he ought not to enjoy it because it was
a human product, yet enjoying it notwithstanding.
He read a few pages on "the progress realized by
modern society," and his reflections ran as follows :

" Let us be humble and believe ourselves in no
way excellent, for we are not excellent.   As we
examine ourselves, let us uncover our true countenance, which is rough and violent like that of our
forefathers, and, as we have the advantage over
them of a longer tradition, let us at least recognize
the sequence and continuity of our ignorance."

Thus pondered M. Bergeret, as he settled himself
in his new abode.   He was not sad, neither was he
glad, as he reflected that he would always yearn in
vain for Madame de Gromance, not realizing the
fact that she was only precious to him by virtue of
the craving which she inspired.   But the very
derangement of his feelings prevented him from

clearly grasping this philosophical truth. He was not handsome, he was not young, he was not rich; he was not sad, because his wisdom approached the happy state of ataraxy, without, however, finally attaining it, and he was not glad, because he was somewhat of a sensualist, and his soul was not free from illusions and desires.

The servant Marie, who had fulfilled her task of bringing terror and misery into the house, had been dismissed, and in her place he had engaged a decent woman from the town, whom he called Angélique, but who was spoken of as Madame Borniche by the shopkeepers and the country-people in the market-place.

Her husband, Nicolas Borniche, a good coach-man, but a bad man, had deserted her when she was still young and ugly. She had been in service with various families. Her status as a married woman still filled her with a certain pride not always con-cealed, and with a great fondness for managing. Finally, she was by way of being a herbalist and a healer, something of a sorceress, and filled the house with a pleasant odour of herbs. Full of genuine zeal, she was obsessed by an eternal longing for affection and approval. From the very first she had taken to M. Bergeret, on account of the distinction of his mind and the gentleness of his manner, but she awaited the arrival of Mademoiselle

Bergeret with foreboding, for a secret presentiment told her that she would not get on well with the sister from Arcachon. On the other hand, she pleased M. Bergeret, who was at last enjoying peace in his house and deliverance from all his troubles.

His books, which heretofore had been despised and thrown about, were now displayed upon long shelves in the big sunny room. There he could work in quiet at his *Virgilius nauticus*, and indulge freely in silent orgies of meditation. Before the window a young plane tree gently waved its pointed leaves, and, farther away, a dark buttress of Saint-Exupère reared its jagged pinnacle, in which grew a cherry tree, doubtless planted there by a bird.

Seated at his table one morning in front of the window, against which the leaves of the plane tree quivered, M. Bergeret, who was trying to discover how the ships of Æneas had been changed into nymphs, heard a tap at the door, and forthwith his servant entered, carrrying in front of her, opossum-like, a tiny creature whose black head peeped out from the folds of her apron, which she had turned up to form a pocket. With a look of anxiety and hope upon her face, she remained motionless for a moment, then she placed the little thing upon the carpet at her master's feet.

" What's that ? " asked M. Bergeret.

It was a little dog of doubtful breed, having something of the terrier in him, and a well-set head, a short, smooth coat of a dark tan colour, and a tiny little stump of a tail. His body retained its puppy-like softness and he went sniffing at the carpet.

"Angélique," said M. Bergeret, "take this animal back to its owner."

"It has no owner, Monsieur."

M. Bergeret looked silently at the little creature who had come to examine his slippers, and was giving little sniffs of approval. M. Bergeret was a philologist, which perhaps explains why at this juncture he asked a vain question.

"What is he called?"

"Monsieur," replied Angélique, "he has no name."

M. Bergeret seemed put out at this answer: he looked at the dog sadly, with a disheartened air.

Then the little animal placed its two front paws on M. Bergeret's slipper, and, holding it thus, began innocently to nibble at it. With a sudden access of compassion M. Bergeret took the tiny nameless creature upon his knees. The dog looked at him intently, and M. Bergeret was pleased at his confiding expression.

"What beautiful eyes!" he cried.

The dog's eyes were indeed beautiful, the pupils of a golden-flecked chestnut set in warm white.

And his gaze spoke of simple, mysterious thoughts, common alike to the thoughtful beasts and simple men of the earth.

Tired, perhaps, with the intellectual effort he had made for the purpose of entering into communication with a human being, he closed his beautiful eyes, and, yawning widely, revealed his pink mouth, his curled-up tongue, and his array of dazzling teeth.

M. Bergeret put his hand into the dog's mouth, and allowed him to lick it, at which old Angélique gave a smile of relief.

"A more affectionate little creature doesn't breathe," she said.

"The dog," said M. Bergeret, "is a religious animal. In his savage state he worships the moon and the lights that float upon the waters. These are his gods, to whom he appeals at night with long-drawn howls. In the domesticated state he seeks by his caresses to conciliate those powerful genii who dispense the good things of this world— to wit, men. He worships and honours men by the accomplishment of the rites passed down to him by his ancestors; he licks their hand, jumps against their legs, and when they show signs of anger towards him he approaches them crawling on his belly as a sign of humility, to appease their wrath."

"All dogs are not the friends of man," remarked

Angélique. " Some of them bite the hand that feeds them."

" Those are the ungodly, blasphemous dogs," returned M. Bergeret, " insensate creatures like Ajax, the son of Telamon, who wounded the hand of the golden Aphrodite. These sacrilegious creatures die a dreadful death or lead wandering and miserable lives. They are not to be confounded with those dogs who, espousing the quarrel of their own particular god, wage war upon his enemy, the neighbouring god. They are heroes. Such, for example, is the dog of Lafolie, the butcher, who fixed his sharp teeth into the leg of the tramp Pied-d'Alouette. For it is a fact that dogs fight among themselves like men, and Turk, with his snub nose, serves his god Lafolie against the robber gods, in the same way that Israel helped Jehovah to destroy Chamos and Moloch."

The puppy, however, having decided that M. Bergeret's remarks were the reverse of interesting, curled up his feet and stretched out his head, ready to go to sleep upon the knees that harboured him.

" Where did you find him ? " asked M. Bergeret.

" Well, Monsieur, it was M. Dellion's *chef* gave him to me."

" With the result," continued M. Bergeret, " that we now have this soul to care for."

" What soul ? " asked Angélique.

" This canine soul. An animal is, properly speaking, a soul ; I do not say an immortal soul. And yet, when I come to consider the positions this poor little beast and I myself occupy in the scheme of things, I recognize in both exactly the same right to immortality."

After considerable hesitation, old Angélique, with a painful effort that made her upper lip curl up and reveal her two remaining teeth, said :

" If Monsieur does not want a dog, I will return him to M. Dellion's *chef ;* but you may safely keep him, I assure you. You won't see or hear him."

She had hardly finished her sentence when the puppy, hearing a heavy van rolling down the street, sat bolt upright on M. Bergeret's knees, and began to bark both loud and long, so that the window-panes resounded with the noise.

M. Bergeret smiled.

" He is a watch-dog," said Angélique, by way of excuse. " They are by far the most faithful."

" Have you given him anything to eat ? " asked M. Bergeret.

" Of course," returned Angélique.

" What does he eat ? "

" Monsieur must be aware that dogs eat bread and meat."

Somewhat piqued, M. Bergeret retorted that in her eagerness she might very likely have taken him away from his mother before he was old enough to leave her, upon which he was lifted up again and re-examined, only to make sure of the fact that he was at least six months old.

M. Bergeret put him down on the carpet, and regarded him with interest.

" Isn't he pretty ? " said the servant.

" No, he is not pretty," replied M. Bergeret. "But he is engaging, and has beautiful eyes. That is what people used to say about me," added the professor, " when I was three times as old, and not half as intelligent. Since then I have no doubt acquired an outlook upon the universe which he will never attain. But, in comparison with the Absolute, I may say that my knowledge equals his in the smallness of its extent. Like his, it is a geometrical point in the infinite." Then, addressing the little creature who was sniffing the waste-paper basket, he went on: " Smell it out, sniff it well, take from the outside world all the knowledge that can reach your simple brain through the medium of that black truffle-like nose of yours. And what though I at the same time observe, and compare, and study ? We shall never know, neither the one nor the other of us, why we have been put into this world, and what we are doing in it. What are we here for, eh ? "

As he had spoken rather loudly, the puppy

looked at him anxiously, and M. Bergeret, returning to the thought which had first filled his mind, said to the servant:

" We must give him a name."

With her hands folded in front of her she replied laughingly that that would not be a difficult matter.

Upon which M. Bergeret made the private reflection that to the simple all things are simple, but that clear-sighted souls, who look upon things from many and divers aspects, invisible to the vulgar mind, experience the greatest difficulty in coming to a decision about even the most trivial matters. And he cudgelled his brains, trying to hit upon a name for the little living thing who was busily engaged in nibbling the fringe of the carpet.

" All the names of dogs," thought he, " preserved in the ancient treatises of the huntsmen of old, such as Fouilloux, and in the verses of our sylvan poets such as La Fontaine—Finaud, Miraut, Briffaut, Ravaud, and such-like names, are given to sporting dogs, who are the aristocracy of the kennel, the chivalry of the canine race. The dog of Ulysses was called Argos, and he was a hunter too, so Homer tells us. ' In his youth he hunted the little hares of Ithaca, but now he was old and hunted no more.' What we require is something quite different. The names given by old maids to their

I

lap-dogs would be more suitable were they not usually pretentious and absurd. Azor, for instance, is ridiculous ! ''

So M. Bergeret ruminated, calling to memory many a dog name, without being able to decide, however, on one that pleased him. He would have liked to invent a name, but lacked the imagination.

" What day is it ? " he asked at last.

" The ninth," replied Angélique, " Thursday, the ninth."

" Well, then ! " said M. Bergeret, " can't we call the dog Thursday, like Robinson Crusoe who called his man Friday, for the same reason ? "

" As Monsieur pleases," said Angélique. " But it isn't very pretty."

" Very well," said M. Bergeret, " find a name for the creature yourself, for, after all, you brought him here."

" Oh, no," said the servant. " I couldn't find a name for him, I'm not clever enough. When I saw him lying on the straw in the kitchen, I called him Riquet, and he came up and played about under my skirts."

" You called him Riquet, did you ? " cried M. Bergeret. " Why didn't you say so before ? Riquet he is and Riquet he shall remain, that's settled. Now be off with you, and take Riquet with you. I want to work."

" Monsieur," returned Angélique, " I am going to leave the puppy with you ; I will come for him when I get back from market."

" You could quite well take him to market with you," retorted M. Bergeret.

" Monsieur, I am going to church as well."

It was quite true that she really was going to church at Saint-Exupère, to ask for a Mass to be said for the repose of her husband's soul. She did that regularly once a year, not that she had ever been informed of the decease of Borniche, who had never communicated with her since his desertion, but it was a settled thing in the good woman's mind that Borniche was dead. She had therefore no fear of his coming to rob her of the little she had, and did her best to fix things up to his advantage in the other world, so long as he left her in peace in this one.

" Eh ! " ejaculated M. Bergeret. " Shut him up in the kitchen or some other convenient place, and do not wor——"

He did not finish his sentence, for Angélique had vanished, purposely pretending not to hear, that she might leave Riquet with his master. She wanted them to grow used to one another, and she also wanted to give poor, friendless M. Bergeret a companion. Having closed the door behind her, she went along the corridor and down the steps.

M. Bergeret set to work again and plunged head foremost into his *Virgilius nauticus*. He loved the work; it rested his thoughts, and became a kind of game that suited him, for he played it all by himself. On the table beside him were several boxes filled with pegs, which he fixed into little squares of cardboard to represent the fleet of Æneas. Now while he was thus occupied he felt something like tiny fists tapping at his legs. Riquet, whom he had quite forgotten, was standing on his hind legs patting his master's knees, and wagging his little stump of a tail. When he tired of this, he let his paws slide down the trouser leg, then got up and began his coaxing over again. And M. Bergeret, turning away from the printed lore before him, saw two brown eyes gazing up at him lovingly.

"What gives a human beauty to the gaze of this dog," he thought, "is probably that it varies unceasingly, being by turns bright and vivacious or serious and sorrowful; because through these eyes his little dumb soul finds expression for thought that lacks nothing in depth nor sequence. My father was very fond of cats, and, consequently, I liked them too. He used to declare that cats are the wise man's best companions, for they respect his studious hours. Bajazet, his Persian cat, would sit at night for hours at a stretch, motionless and majestic, perched on a corner of his table. I still

remember the agate eyes of Bajazet, but those jewel-
like orbs concealed all thought, that owl-like stare
was cold, and hard, and wicked. How much do I
prefer the melting gaze of the dog ! "

Riquet, however, was agitating his paws in
frantic fashion, and M. Bergeret, who was anxious
to return to his philological amusements, said
kindly, but shortly :

" Lie down, Riquet ! "

Upon which Riquet went and thrust his nose
against the door through which Angélique had passed
out. And there he remained, uttering from time to
time plaintive, meek little cries. After a while he
began to scratch, making a gentle rasping noise on
the polished floor with his nails. Then the whining
began again followed by more scratching. Disturbed
by these sounds, M. Bergeret sternly bade him keep
still.

Riquet peered at him sorrowfully with his brown
eyes, then, sitting down, he looked at M. Bergeret
again, rose, returned to the door, sniffed underneath
it, and wailed afresh.

" Do you want to go out ? " asked M. Bergeret.

Putting down his pen, he went to the door, which
he held a few inches open. After making sure that
he was running no risk of hurting himself on the
way out, Riquet slipped through the doorway and
marched off with a composure that was scarcely

polite. On returning to his table, M. Bergeret, sensitive man that he was, pondered over the dog's action. He said to himself:

"I was on the point of reproaching the animal for going without saying either good-bye or thank you, and expecting him to apologize for leaving me. It was the beautiful human expression of his eyes that made me so foolish. I was beginning to look upon him as one of my own kind."

After making this reflection M. Bergeret applied himself anew to the metamorphosis of the ships of Æneas, a legend both pretty and popular, but perhaps a trifle too simple in itself for expression in such noble language. M. Bergeret, however, saw nothing incongruous in it. He knew that the nursery tales have furnished material for nearly all epics, and that Virgil had carefully collected together in his poem the riddles, the puns, the uncouth stories, and the puerile imaginings of his forefathers; that Homer, his master and the master of all the bards, had done little more than tell over again what the good wives of Ionia and the fishermen of the islands had been narrating for more than a thousand years before him. Besides, for the time being this was the least of his worries; he had another far more important preoccupation. An expression, met with in the course of the charming story of the metamorphosis, did not appear suffi-

ciently plain to him. That was what was worrying
him.

"Bergeret, my friend," he said to himself, "this
is where you must open your eyes and show your
sense. Remember that Virgil always expresses
himself with extreme precision when writing on
the technique of the arts ; remember that he went
yachting at Baïae, that he was an expert in naval
construction, and that therefore his language, in
this passage, must have a precise and definite signifi-
cation."

And M. Bergeret carefully consulted a great
number of texts, in order to throw a light upon the
word which he could not understand, and which he
had to explain. He was almost on the point of grasping
the solution, or, at any rate, he had caught a glimpse
of it, when he heard a noise like the rattling of
chains at his door, a noise which, although not
alarming, struck him as curious. The disturbance
was presently accompanied by a shrill whining, and
M. Bergeret, interrupted in his philological investigations, immediately concluded that these importu-
nate wails must emanate from Riquet.

As a matter of fact, after having looked vainly all
over the house for Angélique, Riquet had been
seized with a desire to see M. Bergeret again.
Solitude was as painful to him as human society was
dear. In order to put an end to the noise, and also

because he had a secret desire to see Riquet again, M. Bergeret got up from his arm-chair and opened the door, and Riquet re-entered the study with the same coolness with which he had quitted it, but as soon as he saw the door close behind him he assumed a melancholy expression, and began to wander up and down the room like a soul in torment.

He had a sudden way of appearing to find something of interest beneath the chairs and tables, and would sniff long and noisily ; then he would walk aimlessly about or sit down in a corner with an air of great humility, like the beggars who are to be seen in church porches. Finally he began to bark at a cast of Hermes which stood upon the mantelshelf, whereupon M. Bergeret addressed him in words full of just reproach.

" Riquet ! such vain agitation, such sniffing and barking were better suited to a stable than to the study of a professor, and they lead one to suppose that your ancestors lived with horses whose straw litters they shared. I do not reproach you with that. It is only natural you should have inherited their habits, manners, and tendencies as well as their close-cropped coat, their sausage-like body, and their long, thin nose. I do not speak of your beautiful eyes, for there are few men, few dogs even, who can open such beauties to the light of day. But, leaving all that aside, you are a mongrel, my friend, a

mongrel from your short, bandy legs to your head.
Again I am far from despising you for that. What
I want you to understand is that if you desire to
live with me, you will have to drop your mongrel
manners and behave like a *scolar*, in other words,
to remain silent and quiet, to respect work, after
the manner of Bajazet, who of a night would sit for
four hours without stirring, and watch my father's
pen skimming over the paper. He was a silent and
tactful creature. How different is your own character,
my friend ! Since you came into this chamber of
study your hoarse voice, your unseemly snufflings
and your whines, that sound like steam whistles,
have constantly confused my thoughts and interrupted my reflections. And now you have made me
lose the drift of an important passage in Servius,
referring to the construction of one of the ships
of Æneas. Know then, Riquet, my friend, that
this is the house of silence and the abode of meditation, and that if you are anxious to stay here you
must become literary. Be quiet ! "

Thus spoke M. Bergeret. Riquet, who had
listened to him with mute astonishment, approached
his master, and with suppliant gesture placed a
timid paw upon the knee, which he seemed to
revere in a fashion that savoured of long ago.
Then a kind thought struck M. Bergeret. He picked
him up by the scruff of his neck, and put him upon

the cushions of the ample easy chair in which he was sitting. Turning himself round three times, Riquet lay down, and then remained perfectly still and silent. He was quite happy. M. Bergeret was grateful to him, and as he ran through Servius he occasionally stroked the close-cropped coat, which, without being soft, was smooth and very pleasant to the touch. Riquet fell into a gentle doze, and communicated to his master the generous warmth of his body, the subtle, gentle heat of a living, breathing thing. And from that moment M. Bergeret found more pleasure in his *Virgilius nauticus.*

From floor to ceiling his study was lined with deal shelves, bearing books arranged in methodical order. One glance, and all that remains to us of Latin thought was ready to his hand. The Greeks lay half-way up. In a quiet corner, easy of access, were Rabelais, the excellent story-tellers of the *Cent nouvelles nouvelles,* Bonaventure des Périers, Guillaume Bouchet, and all the old French " conteurs" whom M. Bergeret considered better adapted to humanity than writings in the more heroic style, and who were the favourite reading of his leisure. He only possessed them in cheap modern editions, but he had discovered a poor bookbinder in the town who covered his volumes with leaves from a book of anthems, and it gave M. Bergeret the keenest pleasure to see these free-spoken gentlemen thus

clad in Requiems and Misereres. This was the sole
luxury and the only peculiarity of his austere
library. The other books were paper-backed or
bound in poor and worn-out bindings. The gentle
friendly manner in which they were handled by
their owner gave them the look of tools set out in
a busy man's workshop. The books on archæology
and art found a resting-place on the highest shelves,
not by any means out of contempt, but because
they were not so often used.

Now while M. Bergeret worked at his *Virgilius
nauticus* and shared his chair with Riquet, he found,
as chance would have it, that it was necessary to
consult Ottfried Müller's little *Manual,* which
happened to be on one of the topmost shelves.

There was no need of one of those tall ladders
on wheels topped by railings and a shelf, to enable
him to reach the book; there were ladders of this
description in the town library, and they had been
used by all the great book-lovers of the eighteenth
and nineteenth centuries; indeed, several of the
latter had fallen from them, and thus died honourable deaths, in the manner spoken of in the pamphlet
entitled : *Des bibliophiles qui moururent en tombant de
leur échelle.*

No, indeed ! M. Bergeret had no need of anything of the sort. A small pair of folding steps
would have served his purpose excellently well,

and he had once seen some in the shop of Cléram-
baut, the cabinet-maker, in the Rue de Josde.
They folded up, and looked just the thing with
their bevelled uprights each pierced with a trefoil
as a grip for the hand. M. Bergeret would have
given anything to possess them, but the state of his
finances, which were somewhat involved, forced
him to abandon the idea. No one knew better than
he did that financial ills are not mortal, but, for all
that, he had no steps in his study.

In place of such a pair of steps he used an old
cane-bottomed chair, the back of which had been
broken, leaving only two horns or antennæ, which
had shewn themselves to be more dangerous than
useful. So they had been cut to the level of the
seat, and the chair had become a stool. There
were two reasons why this stool was ill-fitted to the
use to which M. Bergeret was wont to put it. In
the first place the woven-cane seat had grown slack
with long use, and now contained a large hollow,
making one's foothold precarious. In the second
place the stool was too low, and it was hardly
possible when standing upon it to reach the books
on the highest shelf, even with the finger-tips. What
generally happened was that in the endeavour to
grasp one book several others fell out, and it depended
upon their being bound or paper-covered whether

they lay with broken corners or sprawled with leaves spread like a fan or a concertina.

Now with the intention of getting down the *Manual* of Ottfried Müller, M. Bergeret quitted the chair he was sharing with Riquet, who, rolled into a ball with his head tight pressed to his body, lay in warm comfort, opening one voluptuous eye, which he reclosed as quickly. Then M. Bergeret drew the stool from the dark corner where it was hidden and placed it where it was required, hoisted himself upon it, and managed by making his arm as long as possible, and straining upon tiptoe to touch, first with one then with two fingers, the back of a book which he judged to be the one he was needing. As for the thumb it remained below the shelf and rendered no assistance whatever. M. Bergeret, who found it therefore exceedingly difficult to draw out the book, made the reflection that the reason why the hand is a precious implement is on account of the position of the thumb, and that no being could rise to be an artist who had four feet and no hands.

" It is to the hand," he reflected, " that men owe their power of becoming engineers, painters, writers, and manipulators of all kinds of things. If they had not a thumb as well as their other fingers, they would be as incapable as I am at this moment, and they could never have changed the face of the earth as they have done. Beyond a doubt it is the shape of the hand that has assured to man the conquest of the world."

Then, almost simultaneously, M. Bergeret remembered that monkeys, who possess four hands, have not, for all that, created the arts, nor disposed the earth to their use, and he erased from his mind the theory upon which he had just embarked. However, he did the best he could with his four fingers. It must be known that Ottfried Müller's *Manual* is composed of three volumes and an atlas. M. Bergeret wanted Volume I. He pulled out first the second volume, then the atlas, then volume three, and finally the book that he required. At last he held it in his hands. All that now remained for him to do was to descend, and this he was about to do when the cane seat gave way beneath his foot, which passed through it. He lost his balance and fell to the ground, not as heavily as might have been feared, for he broke his fall by grasping at one of the uprights of the bookshelf.

He was on the ground, however, full of astonishment, and wearing on one leg the broken chair; his whole body was permeated and as though constricted by a pain that spread all over it, and that presently settled itself more particularly in the region of the left elbow and hip upon which he had fallen. But, as his anatomy was not seriously damaged, he gathered his wits together; he had got so far as to realize that he must draw his right leg out of the stool in which it had so unfortunately become entangled, and that he must be careful to raise himself up on his right side, which was unhurt. He was even trying to put this into execution when he felt a warm breath upon his cheek, and, turning his eyes, which fright and pain had for the moment fixed, he saw close to his cheek Riquet's little face.

At the sound of the fall Riquet had jumped down from the chair and run to his unfortunate master; he was now standing near him in a state of great excitement; then he commenced to run round him. First he came near out of sympathy, then he retreated out of fear of some mysterious danger. He understood perfectly well that a misfortune had taken place, but he was neither thoughtful nor clever enough to discover what it was; hence his anxiety. His fidelity drew him to his suffering friend, and his prudence stopped him on the very brink of the fatal spot. Encouraged at length by the calm and silence which eventually reigned, he licked M. Bergeret's neck and looked at him with eyes of fear and of love. The fallen master smiled, and the dog licked the end of his nose. It was a great comfort to M. Bergeret, who freed his right leg, stood erect, and limped good-humouredly back to his chair.

Riquet was there before him. All that could be seen of his eyes was a gleam between the narrow slit of the half-closed lids. He seemed to have forgotten all about the adventure that a moment before had so stirred them both. The little creature lived in the present, with no thought of time that had run its course; not that he was wanting in memory, inasmuch as he could remember, not his own past alone, but the far-away past of his ancestors, and his little head was a rich storehouse of useful knowledge; but he took no pleasure in remembrance, and memory was not for him, as it was for M. Bergeret, a divine muse.

Gently stroking the short, smooth coat of his companion, M. Bergeret addressed him in the following affectionate terms:

"Dog! at the price of the repose which is dear to your heart, you came to me when I was dismayed and brought low. You did not laugh, as any young person of my own species would have done. It is true that however joyous or terrible nature may appear to you at times, she never inspires you with a sense of the ridiculous. And it is for that very reason, because of your innocent gravity, that you are the surest friend a man can have. In the first instance I inspired confidence and admiration in you, and now you show me pity.

"Dog! when we first met on the highway of life,

we came from the two poles of creation ; we belong to different species. I refer to this with no
desire to take advantage of it, but rather with a
strong sense of universal brotherhood. We have
hardly been acquainted two hours, and my hand
has never yet fed you. What can be the meaning
of the obscure love for me that has sprung up in
your little heart ? The sympathy you bestow on
me is a charming mystery, and I accept it. Sleep,
friend, in the place that you have chosen ! "

Having thus spoken, M. Bergeret turned over
the leaves of Ottfried Müller's *Manual*, which with
marvellous instinct he had kept in his hand both
during and after his fall. He turned over the pages,
and could not find what he sought.

Every movement, however, seemed to increase
the pain he was feeling.

" I believe," he thought, " that the whole of my
left side is bruised and my hip swollen. I have a
suspicion that my right leg is grazed all over and
my left elbow aches and burns, but shall I cavil
at pain that has led me to the discovery of a
friend ? "

His reflexions were running thus when old Angélique, breathless and perspiring, entered the
study. She first opened the door, and then she
knocked, for she never permitted herself to enter
without knocking. If she had not done so before

K

she opened the door, she did it after, for she had good manners, and knew what was expected of her. She went in therefore, knocked, and said:

" Monsieur, I have come to relieve you of the dog."

M. Bergeret heard these words with decided annoyance. He had not as yet inquired into his claims to Riquet, and now realized that he had none. The thought that Madame Borniche might take the animal away from him filled him with sadness, yet, after all, Riquet did belong to her. Affecting indifference, he replied:

" He's asleep ; let him sleep ! "

" Where is he ? I don't see him," remarked old Angélique.

" Here he is," answered M. Bergeret. " In my chair."

With her two hands clasped over her portly figure, old Angélique smiled, and, in a tone of gentle mockery, ventured:

" I wonder what pleasure the creature can find in sleeping there behind Monsieur ! "

" That," retorted M. Bergeret, " is his business."

Then, as he was of an inquiring mind, he immediately sought of Riquet his reasons for the selection of his resting-place, and lighting on them, replied with his accustomed candour:

"I keep him warm, and my presence affords a sense of security ; my comrade is a chilly and homely little animal." Then he added: "Do you know, Angélique? I will go out presently and buy him a collar."

CHAPTER VII

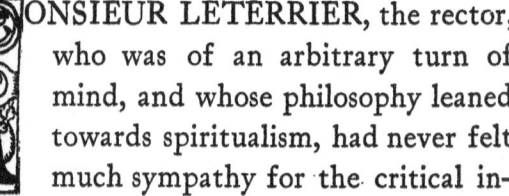ONSIEUR LETERRIER, the rector, who was of an arbitrary turn of mind, and whose philosophy leaned towards spiritualism, had never felt much sympathy for the critical intellect of M. Bergeret. A circumstance, memorable enough, had, however, brought them together. M. Leterrier had taken part in the Affair. He had signed a protest against the verdict, which he conscientiously considered illegal and mistaken. No sooner had he done so than he became the object of public anger and contempt.

The town, which numbered 150,000 inhabitants, only contained five people of the same opinion as himself with regard to the Affair ; these were M. Bergeret, his colleague at the Faculté, two artillery officers, and M. Eusèbe Boulet. The two officers maintained the strictest silence on the subject, and the position of M. Eusèbe Boulet, as editor of the *Phare*, compelled him to express daily, and with no little violence, ideas which were contrary to his convictions, to rail at M. Leterrier, and hold him up to the scorn of all right-minded people.

M. Bergeret had written a letter of congratulation to his rector, and M. Leterrier called upon him.

" Do you not think," said M. Leterrier, " that truth contains a power that renders her invincible, and, sooner or later, ensures her final triumph ? This was the belief of the great Ernest Renan ; it has also been expressed more recently in words worthy to be engraved in bronze."

" It is precisely what I, personally, do not think," returned M. Bergeret. " On the contrary, I opine that in the majority of cases truth is likely to fall a victim to the disdain or insults of mankind and to perish in obscurity. I could give you many instances of this. Remember, my dear sir, that truth has so many points of inferiority to falsehood as practically to be doomed to extinction. To begin with, truth stands alone ; she stands alone as M. l'Abbé Lantaigne says ; for which reason he admires her. But there are no real grounds for such admiration, for falsehood is manifold, and so truth has numbers arrayed against her. That is not her only shortcoming. She is inert, is not capable of modification, is not adapted to those machinations which would enable her to win her way into the hearts and minds of men. Falsehood, on the other hand, possesses the most wonderful resources. She is pliant and tractable, and, what is more (we must not shrink from admitting as much), she is natural and moral. She is natural, as being the product of the working of the senses, the source and fountain-head of all illusion; she is moral, because she fits in with the habits and customs of the human race, who, living in common as they do, founded their ideas of good and evil, their human and divine laws, upon the oldest, most sacred, most irrational, most noble, most barbarous, and most erroneous interpretations of natural phenomena. Falsehood is the principle of all that is beautiful and of good report amongst men. Do we not see winged figures and mythical pictures adorning their gardens, their palaces, and their temples? They lend a willing ear only to the lies of the poets. What makes you wish to destroy falsehood and to seek truth? Such an enterprise can only be inspired by decadent curiosity and culpable intellectual temerity. It is an attempt against the moral nature of man and the laws of society. It is a sin against the sentiments as well as the virtues of the nations. The growth of so great a calamity might well be fatal; were it possible to precipitate matters in that direction, everything would go to rack and ruin. But we know quite well that, as a matter of fact, the progress of truth is very slight and very slow, and encroaches but little upon falsehood."

" You are evidently not here referring to scientific truths," said M. Leterrier. " Their progress is rapid, irresistible, and salutary."

" It is, unfortunately, beyond all question," replied M. Bergeret, " that the scientific verities which penetrate the average mind sink as though in a swamp, and drown. They cause no upheaval and are powerless to destroy error and prejudice. Truths of the laboratory which hold sovereign sway over you and me, Monsieur, have no authority over the minds of the general public. I will mention one example only, to prove this. The system of Copernicus and Galileo is absolutely irreconcilable with Christian philosophy, and yet you know that, both in France itself and the world over, it has penetrated even into the elementary schools without the very smallest modification being made in the theological conceptions it was calculated to annihilate. It is certain that the ideas of a man like Laplace make the old Judæo-Christian cosmogony appear as puerile as the painting upon the dial of a Swiss clock. And yet the theories of Laplace have been clearly exposed for nearly a century without in the least depreciating the value of the little Jewish or Chaldean legends which are still found in the Christian books on religion. Science has never harmed religion, and the absurdity of a religious practice may be clearly demonstrated without lessening the number of the persons who indulge in it. Scientific truths are not acceptable to the public. Nations live on mythology, Monsieur; from legends they draw all the ideas necessary to their existence. They do not need many, and a few simple fables suffice to gild millions of lives. In short, truth has no hold on mankind, and it would be a pity if she had, for her ways are contrary to their nature, as well as to their interests."

"You are like the Greeks, M. Bergeret," said M. Leterrier. "You indulge in fine sophisms, and your reasonings are tuned to the flute of Pan. And yet, I believe with Renan, I believe with Émile Zola, that truth possesses within herself a penetrating force, unknown alike to error and to falsehood. I say 'truth,' and you understand my meaning, M. Bergeret. For the beautiful words, truth and justice, need not be defined in order to be understood in their true sense. They bear within them a shining beauty and a heavenly light. I firmly believe in the triumph of truth; that is what upholds me in the time of trial through which I am now passing."

"And may you be right, Monsieur le Recteur," replied M. Bergeret. "But, generally speaking, I think that the knowledge we have of men and

facts seldom corresponds to the men themselves, or
to the facts accomplished ; that the means by
which our minds can attain this correspondence are
incomplete and insufficient, and that if time reveals
new ways of doing so, it destroys more than it pro-
duces. Madame Roland in prison displayed, to my
mind, a somewhat childlike trust in human justice
when she appealed with so firm a faith and so
confident a mind to impartial posterity. Posterity
is never impartial unless it is indifferent, and what
ceases to interest it it straightway forgets. It is
no judge, as Madame Roland fondly believed. It
is a mob, as blind, wonder-stricken, miserable, and
violent as any other. It has its likes, and, more
especially, its dislikes. It is prejudiced, and lives in
the present, knowing nothing of the past. There is
no such thing as posterity."

"But," objected M. Leterrier, "there is such a
thing as the hour of justice and reparation."

"Do you think," demanded M. Bergeret, "that
the hour of justice and reparation ever sounded for
Macbeth ? "

"Macbeth ? "

"Yes, Macbeth, son of Finleg, King of Scotland.
Two great powers, legend and Shakespeare, have
made of him a criminal. Now I am convinced,
Monsieur, that he was a most excellent man. He
protected the people and the clergy against the

violence of the nobles. He was a thrifty king, a just judge, and the friend of the working classes. History bears witness to it. He did not murder King Duncan; his wife was not a wicked woman. She was called Gruoch, and had three vendettas against the family of Malcolm. Her first husband had been burned alive in his castle. I have here on my table an English review containing materials which prove the goodness of Macbeth and the innocence of his wife. Do you think that if I were to publish these proofs I should succeed in altering public opinion?"

"I do not think so," replied M. Leterrier.

"Neither do I," said M. Bergeret, with a sigh.

At this moment a great clamour arose from the market-place. Some citizens, actuated by zeal for the Army, and in conformity with their recently formed custom, were on their way to break the windows of Meyer the bootmaker.

"*Mort à Zola! Mort à Leterrier! Mort à Bergeret! Mort aux juifs!*" they shouted; and as the rector gave way to some symptoms of distress and indignation, M. Bergeret pointed out to him that he must try and comprehend the enthusiasm of mobs such as this one.

"These people," he said, "are going to break the windows of a bootmaker, and will succeed in doing so without any trouble. Do you think they would be as successful, if, for instance, they had to put in windows or bells at General Cartier de Chalmot's ? No, indeed ! Popular enthusiasm is never constructive, but, on the contrary, essentially destructive. This time it aims at our destruction ; you must not attach too much importance to this particular instance, but rather seek out the laws which govern it."

" No doubt," replied M. Leterrier, who was frankness personified. " But, all the same, these events fill me with consternation. Can we callously look on at the overthrow of justice and truth by a people from whom Europe first learned the law, and who taught the meaning of justice to the whole world ? "

CHAPTER VIII

ONSIEUR LE PREMIER PRÉSI-
DENT CASSIGNOL died in his
ninety-second year, and, in accordance
with his expressed wish, was carried
to his grave upon a pauper's hearse.
This clause in his will was silently condemned. All
present were inwardly offended, as though the in-
junction were intended as a slur upon that object
of universal respect, money, and as the ostentatious
relinquishment of a privilege appertaining to the
bourgeois class. They called to mind that M.
Cassignol had always lived in very good style,
observing, even in extreme old age, a punctilious
nicety with regard to his personal habits, and,
although he had been unceasingly employed in
charitable works, none would ever have dreamed
of saying, in the words of a Christian orator,
" He loved the poor even to becoming as one of
them." They did not believe the thing was done
out of religious zeal, and looked upon it as a paradoxical piece of pride, the elaborate display of
humility being received with the utmost coldness.

They regretted, too, that the deceased, who had been an officer of the Legion of Honour, had directed that no military honours should be paid him. The state of the public mind, inflamed by the nationalist papers, was such, that open complaints at the absence of the military were heard among the crowd. General Cartier de Chalmot, who came in civilian attire, was greeted with profound respect by a deputation of lawyers. A great number of magistrates and clergy thronged around the house of mourning, and when, preceded by the Cross, and to the sound of bells and liturgical chants, the hearse moved slowly towards the cathedral accompanied by twelve white-coiffed nuns, and followed by a long grey and black line of boys and girls from the church schools, which stretched as far as the eye could see, the meaning of this long life entirely consecrated to the triumph of the Catholic Church was at once revealed. The whole town was there. M. Bergeret was among the stragglers following the procession, and M. Mazure, coming up to him, whispered in his ear :

" I knew that old Cassignol had been a fanatical zealot all his life, but I didn't know he was such a prig. He called himself a Liberal ! "

" And so he was," answered M. Bergeret. " He had to be, because his ambition was to govern. Is it not through liberty that we progress along the road to domination ?   My dear M. Mazure, I am indeed sorry for you ! "

" Why ? " asked the keeper of the records.

" Because, being in sympathy with the mob, you constantly display the same pathetic faculty for being deceived, and zealously march along in the procession of triumphant dupes."

" Oh, if you mean the Affair," replied M. Mazure, " I may as well warn you that we shall not agree at all."

" Bergeret, do you know that parson ? " inquired Dr. Fornerol, glancing at a fat and agile priest who was sidling in among the crowd.

" Abbé Guitrel," exclaimed M. Bergeret. " Who does not know of Guitrel and his servant ?   Adventures recounted in days of yore by La Fontaine and Boccaccio are attributed to them. As a matter of fact, the Abbé's servant is of the age stipulated by the canons of the Church. A little while ago this priest, who will soon be a bishop, said something which was retailed to me, and which I in turn repeat to you. He said, ' If the eighteenth century may be called the century of crime, perhaps the nineteenth will be spoken of as the century of atonement.' What do you think of that ? Suppose Guitrel were right."

" No," replied the keeper of the records. " The number of the emancipated increases from day to

day, and liberty of conscience has been set up once
for all. The empire of science has been established.
I am not, however, without some fears of a renewed
attack by the clerical party, present circumstances
favouring reaction. It really worries me, for I am
not, like you, a dilettante. I have a fierce and
anxious love for the Republic."

Chatting thus, they reached the open space in
front of the cathedral. Over the heads of the
people, bald, black, or hoary, the swell of the organ
and the odour of incense were wafted through
the great open doors from the warm twilight
within.

" I'm not going inside," said M. Mazure.

" I will go in for a few minutes," said M. Bergeret.
" I have a taste for ritual."

As he entered, the *Dies Iræ* was rolling out its
spacious phrases. M. Bergeret was behind M.
Laprat-Teulet. On the gospel side, in the part reserved for women, sat Madame de Gromance, lily-
white in her black garments ; her flower-like eyes
void of all thought, which only made her all the
more desirable in M. Bergeret's mind. The
cantor's voice rang out in the great nave, singing
a verse of the funeral chant :

> " Qui latronem exaudisti
> Et Mariam absolvisti
> Mihi quoque spem dedisti."

" You hear, Fornerol," said M. Bergeret, "' *Qui latronem exaudisti*—— Thou, who didst pardon the thief, and absolve the adulteress, hast given hope to me also.' No doubt the recital of such words to a large assembly of people is not without its impressive side, and the praise is due to those untutored and gentle visionaries of the Abruzzi, those humble servants of the poor, those amiable enthusiasts who renounced riches in order to escape from the hatred and ill-will that they engender. They were bad economists, these companions of St. Francis; M. Méline would show his contempt for them, if by any chance he ever heard them spoken about."

" Ah," said the doctor, " the companions of St. Francis were able to look ahead and to see of what material an assembly such as this of to-day would be composed."

" I believe the *Dies Iræ* was written during the thirteenth century in a Franciscan convent," replied M. Bergeret. " I must consult my friend, Commander Aspertini, on the subject."

In the meanwhile the burial service was drawing to a close.

While they followed the hearse that bore the magistrate's remains to the cemetery, M. Mazure, Dr. Fornerol, and M. Bergeret continued their conversation. As they were passing the house of Queen Marguerite, M. Mazure remarked :

"The agreement is signed. M. de Terremondre is owner of the ancient dwelling of Philippe Tricouillard, and intends to house his collection there, in the secret hope of selling it at a tremendous price some day to the town, whose benefactor he will thus become. By the way, Terremondre has made up his mind; he is going to offer himself as progressive republican candidate for Seuilly, but every one knows in what direction his progress will tend. He is a turncoat from the Royalists."

"Hasn't he got the Government behind him?" asked M. Bergeret.

"He is supported by the *préfet*, and opposed by the *sous-préfet*," replied M. Mazure. "The *sous-préfet* of Seuilly is led by the President of the Council, and Worms-Clavelin, the *préfet*, acts upon the instructions of the Minister of the Interior."

"Do you see that shop?" asked the doctor.

"The dyer's and cleaner's shop that belongs to the widow Leborgne?" said M. Mazure.

"Yes," replied Dr. Fornerol. "Her husband died six weeks ago in the most extraordinary way. He literally died of fright and nervous shock at sight of a dog which he believed to be mad, and which was as healthy as I am myself."

At the thought of death M. Mazure, who was

L

a freethinker, felt a sudden longing come over him to possess an immortal soul.

"I do not believe a word of what is taught by the different churches that share in the spiritual guidance of the people," he said. "I know, none better, how dogma is formed, transformed, and elaborated. But why should we not possess a thinking principle, and why should not that principle survive the association of organic elements that we call life ?"

"I should like," replied M. Bergeret, "to ask you what you mean by a thinking principle, but no doubt you would find it difficult to define."

"Not at all," returned M. Mazure. "I give the name to the cause of thought, or, if you prefer it, to thought itself. Why should not thought be immortal ?"

"Yes, why not ?" returned M. Bergeret.

"The supposition is by no means absurd," said M. Mazure, warming to his subject.

"And why," returned M. Bergeret, "should not a certain house in the Tintelleries, bearing the number 38, be inhabited by a M. Dupont ? Such a supposition is by no means absurd. The name of Dupont is common enough in France, and the house of which I am speaking is divided into three parts."

"Now, of course, you're joking!" said M. Mazure.

" In a way I'm a spiritualist," said Dr. Fornerol.
" Spiritualism is a therapeutic agent which must
be reckoned with in the present state of medical
science. All my patients believe in the immortality of the soul, and dislike hearing it ridiculed.
The good people of the Tintelleries quarter and
elsewhere insist on being immortal, and it would
grieve and wound them if anyone were to suggest
anything to the contrary. Madame Péchin, to
wit, coming out of the greengrocer's over there
with a basketful of tomatoes—if you were to go
to her and say: ' Madame Péchin, you will taste
the joys of heaven for hundreds of millions of
centuries, but you are not immortal. You will live
longer than the stars, you will still exist when the
nebulæ have turned into suns, and after the light
of those suns has died ; you will live on in perfect
happiness and glory during inconceivable ages, but
you are not immortal, Madame Péchin ! ' If you
were to say such things to her, she would not look
upon them as good tidings, and if, by chance, your
words were backed up by proofs infallible enough
to convince her, she would be miserable ; the
poor old thing would be in despair, and would
mingle tears with her tomatoes. Madame Péchin
insists on being immortal ; all my patients have a
similar craving. You, M. Mazure, and you, too,
M. Bergeret, have the same desire. Now I will

confess to you that instability is the essential characteristic of the combined elements that go to form life. Shall I give you a scientific definition of life ? It's a damned callous mystery ! "

" Confucius," said M. Bergeret, " was a very sensible man. One day his disciple, Ki-Lou, asked him how to serve the demons and the spirits, to which the master replied, ' Man is not yet in a fit state to serve humanity, so how can he serve the demons and the spirits ? ' ' Permit me,' went on the disciple, ' to ask you what is death.' And Confucius replied, ' We do not know the meaning of life, how, then, can we understand death ? ' "

The procession skirted the Rue Nationale, and passed in front of the college. Dr. Fornerol, being thereby reminded of his youthful days, began :

" That is where I studied. It is a long time ago now. I am much older than either of you. In a week I shall be fifty-six ! "

" And so Madame Péchin really insists on being immortal ? " asked M. Bergeret.

" She is convinced that she is immortal," answered the doctor. " If you told her that she was not, she would take a dislike to you, and disbelieve you all the same."

" And the idea of having to go on for ever amid the universal passing of things does not astonish her ? She does not tire of nourishing such exaggerated hopes ?   Perhaps she has not given much thought to the nature of man and the conditions of life ? "

" What does that matter ? " replied the doctor. " I cannot understand your surprise, my dear M. Bergeret. This good lady is a religious woman; religion, indeed, is her only possession. Having been born in a Catholic country, she is a Catholic, and she believes what she has been taught. It's only nature ! "

" Doctor, you are talking like Zaïre," said M. Bergeret—— " Had I lived on the banks of the Ganges. Besides, the belief in immortality is common in Europe, America, and a part of Asia ; it spreads in Africa with the wearing of clothes."

" So much the better," replied the doctor, " for it is necessary to civilization. Without it the unfortunate would never resign themselves to their fate."

" Yet," retorted M. Bergeret, " the Chinese coolies work for paltry wages. They are patient and resigned, and they are not spiritualists."

" That is because they are yellow," replied the doctor. "The white races have far less resignation. They have conceived an ideal of justice, and formed great hopes. General Cartier de Chalmot is quite right in saying that belief in a future life is necessary to an army. It is also very useful with regard to social intercourse; people would be worse than they are but for the fear of hell."

"Doctor," demanded M. Bergeret, "do you believe you will rise again ? "

"It's different for me," replied the doctor. "I do not find it necessary to believe in God in order to be an honest man. As a scientist I know nothing; as a citizen I believe everything. I am a Catholic by policy, and consider that religious belief is essentially an improving element that helps to humanize the masses."

"That is a very widespread opinion," said M. Bergeret, "and its general acceptance renders it suspect in my eyes. Popular opinions hold good as a matter of course, without analysis, and if they were inquired into, generally speaking they would not pass muster. They are like the theatre-lover who for thirty years was able to attend the plays at the Comédie-Française by simply muttering 'feu Scribe' as he went in, to the man at the ticket-office. If investigated, his right of entry would never have been allowed to pass, but it never was investigated. How can one really believe religion to have a moralizing effect when one reads the history of the Christian nations, and realizes it to be a succession of wars, massacres and tortures. You cannot expect people to be more pious than cloistered monks, and yet monks of every order, black, white, brown, and pied, have been guilty of the most abominable crimes. The agents of the Inquisition and the priests of the League were pious, yet they were cruel. I do not mention the popes who drowned the world in blood, for it is by no means certain that they really believed in a future life. The truth of the matter is that men are evil animals, and remain evil, even when they expect to go from this world into another, which is somewhat unreasonable, when one comes to think of it. All the same, I do not want you to imagine, doctor, that I deny Madame Péchin the right to believe herself immortal. I will even go so far as to say that she will not be disappointed when she departs this life, for a lasting illusion has some of the attributes of truth, and a person who is never disabused is never deceived."

By this time the head of the cortège had entered the cemetery, and the three gossips slackened their pace.

" If you were in my position, M. Bergeret," said the doctor, " and visited each morning a dozen or so of sick folk, you would realize, as I do, the power of the clergy. Come now, do you never find yourself desiring, if not believing in, immortality ? "

" Doctor," replied M. Bergeret, " my thoughts on this subject are the same as those of Madame Dupont-Delagneau. Madame Dupont-Delagneau

was very old when my father was very young. She
was fond of him, and used to enjoy a chat with him ;
she was a link with the eighteenth century. I have
heard him quote her again and again, and this,
amongst others, is an anecdote I have heard him
relate. Once, when she was ill in the country, her
parish priest went to visit her, and began to talk of
a future life.   With a little disdainful grimace, she
retorted that she had her misgivings about the next
world. ' You tell me,' she said, ' that the Creator
of this world made the next too. All I can say is
that I am already too well acquainted with His
handiwork ! ' Thus, doctor, I am at least as mistrustful of the next world as was Madame Dupont-
Delagneau."

"But," asked the doctor, "have you never
dreamed of immortality achieved by science, or life
on another star ? "

"I always come back to the saying of Madame
Dupont-Delagneau," replied M. Bergeret. "I
should be too much afraid that the systems of
Altair or Aldebaran would resemble our solar
system, and that it would not be worth while
changing. And as for being born again on this
terrestrial globe—I think not, doctor, thank you ! "

"But come now, really ! " persisted the doctor.
"Would you not, like Madame Péchin, like to be
immortal, somehow or other ? "

" All things considered," replied M. Bergeret, " I am content with being eternal, and, in my essence, I am that. As for the consciousness I enjoy, that is a mere accident, doctor, a momentary phenomenon, like a bubble formed on the surface of the waters."

"Agreed! But it is better not to say so," replied the doctor.

" Why ? " asked M. Bergeret.

" Because such notions are not suited to the masses, with whom you must agree outwardly, though inwardly you hold other views. It is community of belief that makes strong nations."

" The truth is," replied M. Bergeret, " that men of a common faith have no more urgent desire than to exterminate those who think differently, particularly if the difference is very slight."

" We are going to hear three speeches," said M. Mazure.

He was mistaken. Five speeches were made and no one heard a word. Cries of " *Vive l'armée!* " broke out as General Cartier de Chalmot went by, while Messieurs Leterrier and Bergeret were pursued by the hooting of the youthful Nationalists of the place.

CHAPTER IX

N a wet evening in May, the Brécé
ladies were sitting together in the
big drawing-room, knitting woollen
bodices for the poor children of the
village. Old Madame de Courtrai
was standing with her back to the fire, holding up
her skirts and warming her legs. The Duke, General
Cartier de Chalmot, and M. Lerond were chatting,
prior to a game of whist. The Duke opened the
previous day's paper that was lying upon the table.

"Hostilities between the Americans and the
Spanish have not yet started in earnest," he said.
"What do you anticipate will be the outcome
of it all, General? I should be very glad to have
the opinion of so eminent a military authority as
yourself."

"It would certainly be very instructive if you
would tell us what you think about the forces that
are about to try their strength in the Antilles and
in the China seas, General," put in M. Lerond.

General Cartier de Chalmot passed his hand

164

over his forehead, opened his mouth some time before he spoke, and then said in an authoritative manner:

"The Americans have committed a very imprudent act in declaring war on Spain, and it may well cost them dear. Having no army and no navy, it would be a difficult matter for them to keep up a struggle against an efficient army and a well-trained navy. They have their stokers and their enginemen, but stokers and enginemen do not make a battle fleet."

"Do you think the Spaniards will win, General?" asked M. Lerond.

"Generally speaking, the success of a campaign depends upon circumstances impossible to prophesy," replied the General. "But it may at once be stated that the Americans are not ready for war, and war necessitates long and careful preparation."

"Come, General," cried Madame de Courtrai, "tell us that these American wretches will be beaten!"

"Their success is doubtful," replied the General. "I might even go so far as to say that it would be paradoxical, and an insolent contradiction of every system employed by those nations which are essentially military nations. As a matter of fact, the victory of the United States would constitute a condemnation of the principles adopted throughout

Europe by the most competent soldiers, and such a result is neither likely nor desirable."

"Good!" cried Madame de Courtrai, smacking her withered sides with her bony hands, and shaking her head, with its rough, grey locks that looked like a fur cap. "Good! our friends the Spaniards will be victorious! *Vive le roi!*"

"General," said M. Lerond, "I am most interested in what you say. The success of our friends would be well received in France, and who knows if they might not be the means of stirring up a Royalist and clerical movement in this country!"

"Pardon me," said the General. "I make no prophecy regarding the future. As I have said before, the success of a campaign depends upon circumstances impossible to foresee. All I can do is to take into consideration the quality of the con-flicting elements, and from this point of view the advantage is certainly with Spain, although her fleet does not include a sufficiency of naval units."

"Certain symptoms," said the Duke, "would point to the fact that the Americans have already begun to repent of their temerity. I have heard it positively stated that they are panic-stricken. They live in daily dread of seeing the Spanish ironclads appear on their coasts. The inhabitants of Boston, New York, and Philadelphia are fleeing inland *en masse;* in fact, a general panic exists."

"*Vive le roi!*" repeated Madame de Courtrai, with fierce delight.

"What about little Honorine?" asked M. Lerond. "Is she still favoured with the visitations of Notre-Dame-des-Belles-Feuilles?"

"Yes," replied the dowager duchess, with some embarrassment.

"It would be a good idea," ventured the ex-deputy, "to make an official report of the child's statements of what she sees and hears when in her trances."

No reply was forthcoming to this remark, the reason being that, having undertaken to note down the words attributed by Honorine to the Blessed Virgin, Madame de Brécé very soon stopped doing so: the child's expressions were not nice. Besides, M. le Curé Traviès, who was in the habit of shooting rabbits every evening in the woods of Lénonville, had too often surprised Isidore and Honorine lying among the dead leaves to be any longer in doubt as to why they were there. M. Traviès was something of a poacher, but both his morals and his doctrine were sound. He gathered from repeated observations that it was hardly likely the Blessed Virgin would appear to Honorine.

He had spoken on the matter to the ladies of the castle, who were, if not convinced, at least somewhat perplexed. So when M. Lerond asked them for details of the latest ecstasies, they changed the subject.

" If you care to hear news from Lourdes," said the dowager duchess, " we have some."

" My nephew writes me that many miracles take place in the grotto," said M. de Brécé.

" I have heard the same thing from one of my officers," replied the General. " He is a promising young fellow, and has come back amazed at the wonderful things he saw there."

" You know that the doctors in attendance at the piscina report the most miraculous cures ? " said the Duke.

" We do not need the opinion of learned men to make us believe in miracles," said Madame de Brécé with a limpid smile. " I have far more confidence in the Blessed Virgin than in any doctors."

They then began to talk of the Affair, amazed, so they said, that the " syndicate of treachery " should continue its audacious manifestations unpunished. With much emphasis the Duke expressed himself as follows :

" When two courts martial have given their verdict, the smallest doubt can no longer exist."

" Have you heard," said Madame Jean, " that Mademoiselle Deniseau, the local prophetess, has learned from the mouth of St. Radegonde herself that Zola is going to become a naturalized Italian, and will not return to France?"

This prophecy was received with much favour.

A servant entered, bringing the letters.

"Perhaps there will be some news of the war," said the Duke, opening a paper.

And in dead silence he read the following:

"Commodore Dewey has destroyed the Spanish fleet in the port of Manilla. The Americans have not lost a man."

This telegram caused much depression in the drawing-room. The only person who continued to look confident was Madame de Courtrai, who cried:

"It's not true!"

"The telegram," said M. Lerond, "is an American one."

"Yes," said M. de Brécé, "we must beware of false news."

All endorsed this prudent view of things, and yet were aghast at the sudden vision of a fleet, blessed by the Pope, bearing the flag of His Catholic Majesty, and carrying on the prow of her vessels the names of the Virgin and the saints, disabled, shattered, and sunk by the guns of bacon merchants, sewing-machine manufacturers, and heretics, by a nation without kings, without princes, without a history, without national traditions, and without an army.

CHAPTER X

BERGERET'S affairs were worrying him; he was beginning to fear he might be asked to resign his position at the Faculté, when, to his surprise, he received the intimation that he had been appointed honorary professor there.

The news came to him one day, after his removal to his new rooms in the Place Saint-Exupère, at the very moment when he least expected it. His joy at the event was greater than his progress in ataraxy should have allowed. Vague and flattering hopes arose within him, and when M. Goubin, who had become his favourite pupil since the betrayal of M. Roux, came that same evening to take him for their usual stroll to the Café de la Comédie, he found him beaming all over with smiles.

The night was bright with stars, and as he went along the uneven pavements, M. Bergeret studied the sky. He was interested in the lighter side of astronomy, and pointed out to M. Goubin a beautiful red star over against Gemini.

"That is Mars," he said. "I wish there were

such things as glasses strong enough to see its inhabitants and their industries."

"But, dear Master," said M. Goubin, "were you not telling me some short time ago that the planet Mars was not inhabited, that none of the celestial bodies were inhabited, and that life, such as we conceive it, was a disease confined to our planet alone, a kind of decay spread over the surface of our rotting world?"

"Did I say that?" asked M. Bergeret.

"As far as I can remember that is what you said, dear Master," replied M. Goubin.

And his memory had not played him false. After the betrayal of M. Roux, M. Bergeret had asserted that organic life was but decay eating into the surface of our diseased world. He had also added that he hoped for the greater glory of the heavens that life in the distant worlds produced itself normally, by means of the geometrical forms of crystallization. "Otherwise," he had added, "I could derive no pleasure from the contemplation of the star-spangled sky." Now, however, he was of a different opinion.

"You surprise me," he said to M. Goubin. "There are several reasons for concluding that all those stars now sparkling overhead contain life and thought. Even on this earth of ours, life occasionally has its pleasant side, and thought is divine. I

M

should much like to know something about yon
sister star floating in thin ether in the face of the
sun. She is our neighbour, and only separated
from us by fourteen millions of leagues, which,
astronomically speaking, is a very small distance
indeed. I should like to know if the living beings
upon the planet Mars are more beautiful than we
humans are, and whether their intellect is vaster
than our own."

"That is a thing we shall never know," replied
M. Goubin, wiping his glasses.

"At any rate," went on M. Bergeret, "astrono-
mers have studied the shape of that red planet
by means of powerful telescopes, and they all
agree in saying that they are able to distinguish
innumerable canals upon its surface. Now, the
hypotheses taken as a whole, hypotheses that are
closely interdependent and form a great cosmic
system, lead us to believe that this near neighbour
of ours is older than the earth, from which we may
deduce that her inhabitants, with a longer experience behind them, are wiser than ourselves. The
canals of which I was speaking give to the huge
tracts of land they traverse the appearance of
Lombardy. To be quite correct, we can see
neither the water nor the banks, but only the
vegetation that grows along them, and which, to
the observer, appears as a thin scattered line, pale

or dark according to the season of the year. It is especially to be remarked at the equator of the planet. We give the canals the earthly names of Ganges, Euripus, Phison, Nile, and Orcus. They appear to be irrigating canals, like those at which, it is said, Leonardo da Vinci worked with the skill of an excellent engineer. Their undeviating course, and the circular basins in which they terminate, are sufficient proof that they are both artificial and the result of mathematical calculation. Nature is mathematical, it is true, but not in the same manner.

" The canal which we call Orcus is very wonderful. Its course lies through a number of little round lakes, set at equal distances from one another, which give it the appearance of a rosary. We cannot doubt but that the canals of Mars have been constructed by intelligent beings."

Thus did M. Bergeret people the universe with seductive forms and sublime thoughts. He filled the empty spaces of the boundless heavens because he had been made an honorary professor. He was very wise, but also very human.

When he returned home, he found the following letter awaiting him :

" MILAN.

" DEAR FRIEND,

" You have relied too much upon my knowledge. I am sorry not to be able to satisfy the curiosity which you tell me stirred you during the funeral of M. Cassignol.

"The only interest I have taken in the old Church liturgies lies in their connection in one way and another with the writings of Dante, and I can tell you nothing upon the subject that you do not already know.

"The oldest mention of the chant is made about 1401 by Bartolommeo Pisano. Maroni attributes the *Dies Iræ* to Frangipani Malabranca Orsini, who was cardinal in 1278. Wadding, the biographer of the Franciscan Order Séraphique, ascribes it to Fra Tomaso da Celano, *qui floruit sub anno* 1250. Such attributions are altogether destitute of proof, but it is at any rate probable that it was composed in Italy during the twelfth century.

"In the seventeenth century the defective text of the Roman Missal was further impaired. A marble tablet preserved in the church of San Francesco at Mantua offers an older and more perfect version of the poem. If you would like me to do so, I will have the *Marmor Mantuanum* copied for you. I shall be delighted if you will make use of me in this as in other ways ; nothing would give me more pleasure than to be able to serve you.

"In return, please be good enough to copy for me a letter, written by Mabillon and preserved in the town library ; it is one of the Joliette bequest, collection B, No. 3715⁸, folio 70. The passage that particularly interests me refers to the *Anecdota* of Muratori. Coming from you I shall value it still more.

" It is my opinion, by the way, that Muratori did not believe in God. It has always been my wish to write a book on the atheist-theologians, the number of whom is considerable. Forgive me for the trouble to which I am putting you by asking you to visit the public library ; I trust that you may be rewarded by a meeting with the golden-haired fairy who guards the entrance, and whose dainty ears listen to your flattering remarks the while she swings in her fingers the huge keys that lock away the ancient treasures of your town. Speaking of this fairy reminds me that my days of love are over, and that it is high time for me to cultivate some favourite vice. Life would be sad indeed if the rosy swarm of errant thoughts did not come sometimes to console the old age of the most respectable folk. I am safe in sharing such sound wisdom with a mind as rare and capable of comprehension as your own.

" When you come to Florence I will introduce you to a nymph who guards the house of Dante, and who is well worth your fairy. You will admire her chestnut hair, her black eyes, her full bust, and

her nose you will consider a miracle of loveliness.
It is of medium size, straight and fine, with delicate
nostrils.   I mention this particularly because you
know that nature is not good at noses, and too
often spoils a pretty face by her clumsiness in that
direction.

"Mabillon's letter, which I have asked you to
copy for me, commences thus: 'Ni les fatigues de
l'âge, monsieur . . .' Forgive me for worrying you,
and believe me to be your sincere friend,

"CARLO ASPERTINI.

"P.S.—Why will the French persist in upholding
an error of justice which is now beyond all question,
and which they could quite easily set right without
harming anyone ?   I can find no solution to their
conduct in this matter.   All my countrymen, all
Europe, and the whole world share my amazement.
I should very much like to have your opinion
regarding this extraordinary affair.

"C. A."

CHAPTER XI

N the clear light of early morning the quarters were full of the passing to and fro of the men on duty, sweeping the cobbles, or grooming down the horses. At the far end of the yard, clothed in his canvas trousers and dirty blouse, stood Private Bonmont, with his comrades, Privates Cocot and Briqueballe, peeling potatoes in front of a cauldron full of water. Now and then a squad, under the conduct of a non-commissioned officer, rushed down the stairs like a torrent, scattering on its way the invincible gaiety of the young.

The most characteristic feature of these men who had been taught to march was their step, a heavy, laboured step, crushing and sonorous. Important-looking pay-sergeants continually passed by with account-books of all sizes under their arms. Privates Bonmont, Cocot and Briqueballe were peeling potatoes and throwing them into the cauldron, and as they did so they gave vent to the most harmless of thoughts in words that were few

but of an exceeding coarseness. Private Bonmont
was thinking deeply.

In front of him, beyond the barrack gates that
closed in the courtyard of the huge building,
stretched a circle of hills with villas nestling in the
purple branches of the trees, and sparkling in the
morning sun. There resided the actresses and light
women brought to the town by the presence of Private
Bonmont. A whole swarm of women, bookmakers,
journalists belonging to sporting and military papers,
jockeys, procurers, male and female, and swindlers of
all descriptions, had settled down in the vicinity of
the barracks where the rich conscript was serving
his time. As he peeled the potatoes, he might have
congratulated himself on being able to bring
together so Parisian a society at so great a distance
from Paris. But he knew life well and men better,
so his pride was in no way flattered by the achieve-
ment. He was worried and morose. Life held only
one ambition for him, and that was the badge of
the Brécé Hunt. He longed for it with inherited
tenacity, with the forcefulness that his father, the
great Baron, had shown in his conquest of souls,
bodies, and things, but not with the deep, clear-
sighted thought or genius of his stupendous parent.
He felt himself inferior to his wealth ; this made
him unhappy, and, in consequence, spiteful.

" They only give their blessed badge to dukes

and peers, I know," he reflected. "The Brécés are overrun with Americans and Jewesses, and I'm as good as they any day ! "

He threw his peeled potato angrily into the cauldron, at which Private Cocot, with a big laugh and a big oath, cried out :

" There he goes, upsetting the broth, damn him ! "

And Briqueballe, who was a simple soul, and of the same year, made merry at the jest. He rejoiced, too, at the thought that he would soon see his father, who was a harness-maker at Cayeux, and his home again.

" That old hypocrite Guitrel will do nothing for me," thought Private Bonmont. " He is a clever chap is Guitrel, cleverer than I ever thought. He has made his own conditions. So long as he is not bishop he will not say anything to his friends, the Brécés. He is a deep beggar, and no mistake ! "

" Bonmont," said Briqueballe, " stop chucking the peelings into the pot ! "

" It's a dirty trick ! " said Cocot.

" I'm not on duty this week," objected Bonmont.

Thus spoke these three men because they were on an equal footing.

Bonmont went on thinking :

" I can do without Guitrel. There are plenty of others who will get the badge for me. Terre-

mondre, for instance; he knows the Brécés
well. His family is quite good, and he's all right
—but not to be relied upon; he's a dodger, a
regular dodger! He'll promise everything and do
nothing."

"I couldn't very well ask old Traviès, who goes
out helping Rivoire the poacher. There is General
Cartier de Chalmot; he'd only have to open his
mouth—but the old crock hates me."

These were Private Bonmont's opinions, and they
were not altogether unfounded. General Cartier
de Chalmot did not like him. "If little Bonmont
were under me I'd make him sit up," he was in
the habit of saying. As for the General's wife, her
indignation regarding him knew no bounds since
the day she had heard him say at a ball: "Putting
all sentiment aside, mother is too damned lazy."
No, young Bonmont was not mistaken, it was no
good looking for help either from the General or
his wife.

He searched his memory to try and discover
some one to render him the service which Guitrel had
refused him. M. Lerond? He was too cautious.
Jacques de Courtrai? He was in Madagascar.

Young Bonmont heaved a deep sigh. As he peeled
his last potato a sudden inspiration came to him.

"Supposing I made Guitrel a bishop! That
would be rich!"

As this idea flashed through his brain a torrent of curses sounded in his ears.

"*Nom de Dieu! Nom de Dieu! Misère de misère!*" yelled Briqueballe and Cocot, as a shower of soot fell suddenly upon them, around them, and into the cauldron, soiling their wet fingers, and blackening the potatoes, which a moment before had been ivory white.

Looking up to seek the cause of their trouble, they espied through the black shower some of their comrades upon the roof removing a long chimney flue, and shaking out the soot with which it was filled. As they caught sight of them, Cocot and Briqueballe cried as with one voice:

"Hi! you up there! what the devil are you doing?"

And they hurled at their comrades all the curses their simple souls could conjure up. They were innocent curses, full of genuine anger, and they filled the barrack yard with echoes in the accents of Picardy and Burgundy. Then the face of Sergeant Lafile, with its slight moustache, appeared over the edge of the roof, and, amid the sudden silence, a sarcastic voice rasped out these words:

"Three days for you two down there. Do you understand?"

Briqueballe and Cocot stood overwhelmed by

the hard blows of fate and discipline, while their companion, Private Bonmont, reflected :

" I can make a bishop right enough. I've only got to speak to Huguet, and it's done ! "

Huguet was then president of the council. His cabinet was a moderate one, supported by the Conservatives. When forming it, Huguet had been careful to safeguard capital, gaining thereby a calm self-confidence and not a little pride. He was Minister of Finance, and was supposed to have given stability to the public credit, which had been shaken by his Radical predecessor.

He had not always been so clever a statesman. He had been a Radical in his hard-working youth, a Radical, and a revolutionary even. He had been private secretary to the late Baron de Bonmont, for whom he wrote books and edited papers. In those days he was a democrat, and a dreamer in matters of finance. That was the baron's wish, for the great man was anxious to conciliate the progressive factions of Parliament, and therefore liked to appear generous and even something of a dreamer too. This was what he called " giving himself room." It was he who made his secretary member for Montil; Huguet owed everything to him, and young Bonmont realized all this.

" I shall only have to say the word to Huguet," he thought. That was how he put it to himself, at any rate. But he was not really sure of it, for he knew that M. Huguet, President of the Council, was careful to avoid any encounter with Private Bonmont, and did not like to be reminded of the old ties that had associated him with the great baron, who had died so opportunely, amid dawning rumours of scandal. So, on second thoughts, Private Bonmont sagely decided that it would be necessary to find some one else.

He sat down upon the ground beside the pump, that he might be able to think more at his ease, and was soon lost in meditation. In his imagination every person who might, he thought, prove capable of disposing of the episcopal crozier and mitre filed in a long procession before him. Monseignor Charlot, M. de Goulet, Worms-Clavelin, the *préfet*, Madame Worms-Clavelin, and M. Lacarelle crossed his mental vision, and many others beside. He was awakened from his reverie by Private Jouvencie, licentiate in law, pumping water down his back.

" Jouvencie," said Bonmont solemnly, wiping his neck, " what is Loyer minister of ? "

" Loyer ? Minister of Public Instruction and Public Worship," replied Jouvencie.

" Does he appoint the bishops ? "

" Yes."

" You are sure ? "

" Yes, why ? "

" Oh, nothing," replied Bonmont.

But to himself he said :

" I've got it—Madame de Gromance ! "

CHAPTER XII

HAT same evening M. Leterrier came to see M. Bergeret.

At the sound of the bell Riquet leapt down from the couch he was sharing with his master, and, with one eye on the door, set up a terrific barking. When M. Leterrier came into the room, the dog received him with hostile growls; the portly form and full, grave countenance fringed with grey beard, were not familiar to him.

"You too!" murmured the rector gently.

"Please excuse him," said M. Bergeret. "He is a domesticated animal. When men undertook the training of his forefathers, and, in so doing, formed the characteristics he has inherited, they themselves regarded a stranger as an enemy. They did not inculcate in dogs charity towards the human race. Thoughts of universal brotherhood have not entered the soul of Riquet; he stands for the old order of things."

"And a very ancient one," replied the rector,

" for it is, of course, clear that nowadays we live in unity, peace and concord, with one another ! "

He spoke these words with a bitterness not natural to him, but for some time past his thoughts and speech had changed.

However, Riquet continued to bark and growl ; he was evidently doing his best to scare away the stranger by his voice and fearsome appearance, but, as fast as the enemy advanced, he retreated. He was a faithful house-dog, but cautious withal.

At last his master, growing impatient, picked him up by the scruff of the neck, and gave him two or three taps on his nose, whereupon Riquet immediately stopped barking, wriggled, and put out a pink, curling tongue to lick the hand that had chastised him, his beautiful eyes full of gentle sadness the while.

" Poor Riquet," sighed M. Leterrier, " that is all you get for your zeal."

" I must drive things into his head," replied M. Bergeret, pushing him behind him at the back of his chair. " Now he knows he was wrong to greet you in such fashion. Riquet conceives of one evil only, physical suffering, and of but one happiness, the absence of suffering. He identifies crime and punishment, inasmuch as for him a misdeed is a deed that is punished. If by accident I step on his paw, he feels himself to be the guilty party, and begs my pardon ; justice and injustice do not trouble his infallible wisdom."

" Such philosophy spares him the mental anguish some of us are experiencing to-day," said M. Leterrier.

Since the day he had signed the protest of the " Intellectuals " M. Leterrier lived in a state of perpetual astonishment. He had set forth his reasons in a letter to the local newspapers, and could not understand his opponents who called him a Jew, a Prussian, an " Intellectual," and said that he had been bought. What also surprised him was that Eusèbe Boulet, the editor of the *Phare*, referred to him daily as a disloyal citizen and an opponent of the Army.

" Would you believe it ? " he cried. " They have dared to put in the *Phare* that I insult the Army ! *I* insult the Army ! I who have a son serving with the colours ! "

The two professors spoke at length of the Affair, and M. Leterrier, of the still guileless soul, repeated:

" I cannot understand why political considerations and party passions should be brought into the affair at all. It is a question of moral right, and far above such things ! "

" Exactly ! " replied M. Bergeret. " But you would not be in a state of perpetual astonishment if you would only remember that the passions of

N

the mob are simple and violent, and that it is impossible to reason with such people. Few men are clever enough to keep control of their minds during difficult investigations, and it has required sustained attention on our part to discover the truth of the matter. It has required sustained attention, and the force of minds trained to the examination of facts with method and sagacity. Advantages such as these, and the satisfaction of knowing oneself in possession of them are well worth a few contemptible insults."

" When will it all end ? " asked M. Leterrier.

" In six months, perhaps, or twenty years—o never," replied M. Bergeret.

" Where will they draw the line ? " asked M. Leterrier. " *Scelere velandum est scelus.* It is killing me, my friend, it is killing me ! "

It was true. His sense of right and wrong had gone awry, he was feverish and his liver was out of order.

For the hundredth time he expounded the proofs which he had amassed, with all the prudence of his mind and all the zeal of his heart. He exposed the first causes of the error, which slowly but surely appeared behind the masses of untruth which had veiled it. Then, strong in the conviction of right, he vigorously demanded :

" What answer can they give ? "

At this point of the conversation the two professors heard a great clamour rising from the street. Riquet lifted up his head and listened anxiously.

" What is it now ? " asked M. Leterrier.

" It is nothing," replied M. Bergeret, " only Pecus ! "

It was, indeed, as he had said a crowd of people uttering loud cries.

" I think I hear ' *Conspuez Leterrier!* ' " said the rector. " They must have heard that I am here ! "

" I think so too," said M. Bergeret, " and I believe that they'll soon be shouting ' *Conspuez Bergeret!* ' Pecus is fed on ancient ideas, and his aptitude for error is considerable. Feeling himself incapable of bringing reason to bear upon hereditary prejudices, he prudently sticks to the heritage of nursery tales, handed down by his forefathers. This particular kind of wisdom preserves him from errors that would otherwise do him harm. He keeps to the old and tried errors. He is imitative, and would be more so, were it not that he involuntarily deforms everything he imitates, such deformations going by the name of progress. Pecus never thinks, and it is unjust to say that he deceives himself. To his unhappiness, be it said, everything combines to deceive him. He knows not the meaning of doubt, for doubt springs from thought. Yet his ideas are ever changing, and at times his stupidity turns to violence. He excels in nothing, for everything that is in any way excellent flies before him, and ceases to be his. He wanders and languishes and suffers. We must give him deep, sorrowful sympathy; we must even venerate him, for it is from him that all virtue, all beauty, and all human glory spring. Poor Pecus ! "

As M. Bergeret was pronouncing these words, a stone came hurtling through the window and fell upon the floor.

" There is an argument ! " said the rector, picking up the stone.

" And rhomboid in shape," said M. Bergeret.

" It bears no inscription," said the rector.

" That is a pity ! " answered M. Bergeret. " Commander Aspertini found at Modena some sling stones used by the soldiers of Hirtius and of Pansa against the followers of Octavius, in the year 43 B.C. These stones bore inscriptions, indicating whom they were intended to strike. M. Aspertini showed me one destined for Livy. I leave you to guess in what form the soldier's humour couched the terms of the inscription."

His voice was drowned at this point by cries of " *Conspuez Bergeret ! Mort aux juifs !* " which rose from the square.

Taking the stone from the hands of the rector,

M. Bergeret placed it upon his table to serve as a letter-weight, and as soon as he could hear himself speak, went on with his remarks :

" Horrible cruelties were committed after the defeat of the two consuls at Modena. It cannot be denied that society has improved since then."

The crowd went on yelling, however, and Riquet replied to it with heroic barks.

CHAPTER XIII

EING in Paris on sick leave, young Bonmont went to see the Automobile Exhibition that was being held near the Terrasse des Feuillants, in the Jardin des Tuileries. As he walked down one of the side galleries reserved for parts and accessories, he examined the Pluto Carburettor, the Abeille Motor, and the Alphonse Lubricator, with an unenthusiastic eye and a weary curiosity. With a curt nod or wave of the hand he returned the greetings of timid young men and obsequious old ones. He was neither proud nor triumphant, but simple, rather common-looking, and armed only with the undeviating and tranquil air of malevolence that stood him in such good stead in his dealings with men; he went his way, a short, hunched-up, rather hump-backed little figure, broad-shouldered, strong and vigorous enough, although already attacked by disease.

He went down the steps of the terrace, and while examining the trade-marks distinguishing the

different lubricating oils, he came upon one of
the statues of the gardens, which had been shut in
the tent enclosure ; it was a classical study in the
French style, a bronze hero whose academic nudity
displayed the sculptor's skill, and who in a fine
gymnastic attitude was felling a monster to the
ground.   Misled, no doubt, by the apparently
sporting air of the group, and never reflecting that
the statue had probably been in the garden long
before the Exhibition, Bonmont instinctively began
to wonder what connexion it could have with
motoring. He thought that the monster, a serpent,
which, as a matter of fact, did look like a tube, was
intended to represent a pneumatic tyre, but his
thoughts were very hazy and confused. He turned
aside his lack-lustre gaze almost immediately, and
entered the great hall where the cars on platforms
complacently displayed the clumsy, imperfectly developed, and still ill-balanced forms which at the
same time struck the onlooker with an irritating
impression of self-satisfaction and conceit.

Young Bonmont was not enjoying himself there ;
he never enjoyed himself anywhere. But he might
have found a certain pleasure in inhaling the odour
of rubber and oils that filled the air ; he might have
examined the autocars and autolettes with a little
interest, but that for the moment he was possessed
by one single idea. He was thinking of the Brécé

Hunt, and the longing to obtain the badge filled his very soul. From his father he had inherited this tenacious will and the burning intensity with which he coveted the Brécé badge was mingled in his veins with the fever of incipient phthisis. He longed for it with all the impatience of a child—for his mind was still very childish—and he longed for it with the cunning tenacity of a calculating and ambitious man—for he knew human nature well, having in a few years learned many things.

He knew that, as far as the Duc de Brécé was concerned, he, with his French name and his Roman title, was still Gutenberg, the Jew. He also realized the power of his millions, and he knew more upon this subject than will ever be grasped by peoples or their rulers. So he was neither deluded nor discouraged. He took in the situation accurately, for he was clear-headed. True the anti-Jewish campaign had been conducted with the utmost vehemence in agricultural districts like his own, which contained no Jews, but a large number of clergy. Recent events and the newspaper articles had been a great strain upon the feeble head of the Duc de Brécé, the leader of the Catholic party in his Department. Doubtless, the Bonmonts were of the same way of thinking as the grandsons of *émigrés*, and were as full of Royalist devotion and quite as zealous Catholics as himself. But the Duke could not forget their origin—he was a simple, obstinate man, and young Bonmont was well aware of this. He reviewed the situation once again in front of the Dubos-Laquille motor omnibus, and came to the conclusion that the best way of obtaining the de Brécé badge was to procure the bishop's crozier for M. l'Abbé Guitrel.

"I must have him nominated," he reflected. "It is absolutely necessary. It will be easy enough once I know how to set about it." And, full of regret, he added, "Father would have advised me in the matter if he had lived. He must have made more than one bishop in Gambetta's time."

Although he was not quick at generalisation, he went on to remind himself that anything could be bought for money, a thought which imbued him with great confidence in the success of his enterprise. Reflecting thus, he looked up and saw young Gustave Dellion a little in front of him, looking at a yellow-wheeled car.

Dellion caught sight of Bonmont at the same moment, but pretending he had not seen him, he beat a retreat behind the body of the vehicle. He was under long-standing financial obligations to Bonmont, and, for the present, was in no way prepared to discharge them. The mere sight of his friend's blue eye gave him a hollow feeling in the pit of his stomach, for it was Bonmont's habit to stare silently and terribly at those of his friends who owed him money. Dellion knew all about that, and was much surprised when the little bull, as he termed him, joined him in his retreat between the canvas wall of the tent and the yellow-wheeled car, holding out a friendly hand, and saying with a pleasant smile :

" How are you ? Nice car ! A bit long in the body, but not so bad, is it ? That's what you want for Valcombe, my dear Gustave. Yes, indeed ! There's a pretty puff-puff that would rip along nicely between Valcombe and Montil."

The mechanic who was standing by the motor thought good to intervene, and to point out to M. le Baron that the vehicle could be turned into an open six-seater, or a closed phaeton with seats for four. Seeing that he was dealing with connoisseurs, he launched out into technical explanations.

" The motor is composed of two horizontal cylinders ; each piston works a crank inclined at 180° to its neighbour."

In businesslike terms he demonstrated the advantages of such a combination. Then, in answer to a question by Gustave Dellion, he said that the carburettor was automatic, and to be regulated once for all at the moment of starting.

He stopped speaking, and the two young fellows stood there silent and attentive. At last, pushing his stick between the spokes of one of the wheels, Gustave Dellion remarked:

"Do you see, Bonmont? Steering is done by differential gear!"

"It is very easy to handle," said the mechanic.

Gustave Dellion loved an automobile, and not, like Bonmont, with an already satiated love. He gazed at the vehicle which, in spite of the stiffness of modern body-work, looked like a great animal, a conventional, banal, though well-behaved monster, with an apology for a head between the lamps that looked like two huge eyes.

"Not such a bad puff-puff," whispered young Bonmont to his friend. "Why don't you buy it?"

"Buy it? Can you do anything you like when you are so unfortunate as to possess a father!" sighed Gustave Dellion. "You don't know what a nuisance a family is—what a worry." Then, with feigned assurance, he added, "And that, my dear Bonmont, reminds me that I owe you a small——"

A friendly hand fell upon his shoulder, cutting him short, and to his surprise there stood at his side a little fair man, his head sunk between his shoulders, giving him the appearance of a slight hump, broad-chested, and strong-backed—a little, simple-looking, fair man, who regarded him with extraordinarily kind blue eyes and a sweet smile.

" You old fool ! " said this little man, suggesting a good-natured little buffalo shedding his wool on the bushes out of pure kindness of heart.

Gustave no longer recognized the Bonmont he had known, and was both touched and surprised. Jumping into the car, the little Baron began to handle the steering-wheel under the benevolent eye of the mechanic.

" So you drive, Bonmont ? " ventured Gustave with deference.

" Occasionally," returned young Bonmont.

Then, with one hand upon the steering-wheel, he related a motor-tour he had made in Touraine during one of his absences on sick leave, from which he always returned worse than he went away. He had done thirty miles an hour. Of course, the roads were dry and in good condition, but there were cattle, children, and frightened horses to pass, all of which might have caused trouble. You had to keep your eyes about you, and never let the other fellow touch the wheel. He related a few incidents of the tour, one adventure with a milkwoman standing out particularly in his mind.

" I saw the old woman coming along," he said, " taking up the whole of the road with her horse and cart. I sounded my horn, but the old creature never moved aside. Then I made straight for her. She was new to that trick. She drew up by the side of the road, pulling so hard at her horse that he fell in a heap with the cart, milk-pails, old woman and all, upon a pile of stones; so I left them to it and went on," concluded young Bonmont, as he jumped out of the car. " And, in spite of the dust and the noise, motoring is a very pleasant way of getting about. You try it, my dear fellow."

" He is a good sort, after all," thought young Dellion admiringly. And his wonder grew when, dragging him along by the arm through the great hall, Bonmont said to him :

" You are quite right. Don't buy that motor. I'll lend you my runabout. I shan't want it, because I've got to go back, my leave is nearly up. Besides—— By the way, do you know if Madame de Gromance is in Paris ? "

" I believe so, but I am not quite sure," replied Gustave. " It is some time since I saw her."

This was in one way an honourable falsehood, for at ten minutes past seven on the preceding evening he had left Madame de Gromance in her room at the hotel where they had their rendez-vous.

Bonmont did not reply, but, coming to a full stop before a notice in two languages, forbidding smoking, he gazed at it silently and thoughtfully. Gustave, following his example, remained speechless, thinking it would not be prudent to bring the interview to an end. So he added:

" But I may see her again soon. I *can* see her, if you will tell me——"

The little Baron looked him straight in the eyes, and said:

" Would you like to do me a favour ? "

Gustave assented with the enthusiasm of a good-natured soul and the uneasiness of a person suddenly embarked upon a difficult enterprise. It was none the less true that Gustave could do Ernest de Bonmont a favour, and the latter proceeded to enlighten him on the subject.

" If you would like to do me a favour, my dear Gustave, get Madame de Gromance to go and see Loyer, and ask him to make Abbé Guitrel a bishop." And he added, " You would do me a genuine service."

To this request Gustave replied by a stupefied silence and a startled look, not that he intended to refuse, but because he had not grasped the situation. Young Bonmont had to repeat the same words twice over, and to explain that Loyer was Minister of Public Worship and nominated the bishops. He was very patient, and little by little Gustave understood what was required of him ; he even managed to repeat what he had heard without making a single mistake:

" You want me to tell Madame de Gromance
to go and ask Loyer, who is Minister of Public
Worship, to make Guitrel a bishop ? "

" Bishop of Tourcoing."

" Tourcoing ! Is that in France ? "

" Of course."

" Ah ! " said Gustave thoughtfully, and he fell
into a reverie.

Serious objections came to him, and, at the risk
of appearing disobliging, he would mention them.
It seemed to him that the request entailed a good
deal, and he did not want to enter upon it lightly.
Timidly and hesitatingly he formulated his first
objection, which was a natural one.

" It isn't a trick, is it ? " he asked.

" What do you mean by a trick ? " said Bonmont
shortly.

" No, really," protested Gustave, " you aren't
pulling my leg ? "

He was still in doubt, but the contemptuous look
of the little fair man dispersed all doubt.

With great firmness and decision he declared :

" As long as I know it is a serious matter, you can
rely upon me. I can be serious when necessary."

He was silent awhile, and the difficulties con-
fronting him again rose in his mind. Gently and
timidly he said :

" Do you think that Madame de Gromance

knows the minister well enough to ask such a—a—
favour ? Because, you know, she never mentions
Loyer to me."

" And that," replied the little Baron, " is probably because she has other subjects to discuss with
you. I don't mean that she is keen on Loyer, but
she thinks him a good old sort, and no fool. They
got to know each other three years ago on the platform at the unveiling of the statue to Jeanne d'Arc.
Loyer would be only too delighted to do anything to
please Madame de Gromance, and I can assure you
he isn't a bad sort. When he puts on his best coat
he looks like a retired fencing-master. She can go
and see him all right, he will be quite nice to her
—and he will most certainly do her no harm ! "

" In that case," said Gustave, " she is to ask him
to make Guitrel a bishop."

" Yes."

" Bishop of where did you say ? "

" Bishop of Tourcoing," repeated young Bonmont. " I'd better write it down for you."

Picking up from a table before him the trade
card of the builder of the " Reine des Pygmées,"
he wrote upon it with his little gold pencil, " Make
Guitrel Bishop of Tourcoing."

Gustave took the card, and the idea which at
first had appeared to him so strange and weird
now seemed a simple and natural one. His mind

had grown accustomed to it, and as he put the
card in his pocket he repeated in the glibbest
way :

"Make Guitrel Bishop of Tourcoing. Right you
are ! You can rely on me."

In this manner the words of Madame Dellion were
fulfilled, who speaking of her son one day had
said, " Gustave does not learn quickly, but he re-
members what he has learned, and that is perhaps
best."

"You know," said Ernest seriously, " I can
answer for Guitrel making a good bishop."

"So much the better," replied Gustave, " because——" And he did not finish his sentence.

They had now reached the exit, however.

" I shall be in Paris until the end of the week,"
said Bonmont. " Let me know how things are
going ; there is no time to lose, for the candidates
are being chosen now. We will speak of the car
at another time."

As they reached the flight of flag-decorated steps,
he took Gustave's hand in his and, holding it, impressed upon him :

" No one must know. The thing is of the utmost
moment, my dear Dellion, that no one shall know ;
not a soul must know that Madame de Gromance
is going to Loyer at your request. Now that is
understood, is it not ? "

o

" Quite," replied Gustave, heartily shaking his friend's hand.

The same evening at eight o'clock young Bonmont went to visit his mother, whom he did not often see, but with whom he was on the friendliest possible terms, and found her finishing her toilet in the dressing-room.

While her maid was arranging her hair she looked away from her reflection in the glass, and turning to her son :

" You don't look well," she said.

Ernest's health had been worrying her for some time. Rara provided her with other more painful worries, but her son was, for all that, a source of anxiety.

" How are you, mother ? "

" Oh, I'm very well."

" You look it."

" Did you know that your Uncle Wallstein has had a slight stroke ? "

" I'm not surprised ; he shouldn't be so gay at his time of life, it's unnatural."

" He is not so very old, only fifty-two."

" Fifty-two is not what you might call youthful, exactly. By the way, what about the Brécés ? "

" The Brécés ? What about them ? "

" Did they thank you for the ciborium ? "

" They sent their card, with a pencilled word of thanks."

" That's not much."

" Well, *mon petit*, what else did you expect ? "

She rose to her feet and raised her hands above her head to fix a diamond cluster in her hair; standing thus her bare arms looked like two handles springing from a beautifully shaped amphora. Her shoulders gleamed under the electric light which shone through transparent shades shaped like bunches of fruit, and in the golden whiteness of the skin delicate blue veins ran down to the swell of her bosom. Her cheeks were rouged and her lips painted, but her face was still youthful in its health and vigour. The lines of her neck, which might have betrayed the passage of the years, were lost in the beauty of the skin.

Young Bonmont studied her carefully for a few moments, and then said :

" Mother, suppose you go and see Loyer too, and ask him about Abbé Guitrel ? "

CHAPTER XIV

ADAME DE BONMONT, who had chosen Raoul Marcien from among all others, and who loved him with deep affection, was justified for the space of a few weeks in congratulating herself upon her choice, and in believing herself a happy woman. A tremendous change had taken place in the order of things. Raoul, who had formerly been despised or disliked in all circles of society, who had been rejected by his regiment, cut by his friends, cast off by his relations, expelled from his club ; who was known in all the courts of law by reason of the repeated charges of swindling brought against him, had suddenly become cleansed of all stain and purified of all dishonour. Certain events, guessed at, no doubt, and soon to be made clear, had interested the Government on his behalf. It was exceedingly necessary that Raoul should pass for an honourable man. In public and in private, ministers maintained that the power and glory of France and the peace of the whole world depended upon this,

His honour was of public utility, and each and all did their best to make it an established fact. The Government worked to this end, as did the lawyers and the newspapers, in fact all good citizens worked joyfully for its establishment. Madame de Bonmont experienced both pleasure and uneasiness at the sudden transformation of her lover into an example and a model for all Frenchmen. She was made for the enjoyment of tranquil joys and pleasures *à deux*, and all this fame astonished and made her ill at ease. When with Raoul she had the fatiguing sensation of living perpetually in a lift.

Evidences of the esteem in which he was held amazed the simple Elizabeth both by their number and extent. Congratulations, flattering pledges, good-conduct certificates, compliments, and praises poured in from all the bodies known and unknown, and from all the public societies in town and country. They came from the courts, the barracks, the archbishops' palaces, from the town halls, *préfectures* and great houses of France. They rang out in the street riots, and resounded with the bugles during torchlight processions. His honour shone proudly forth nowadays ; it flamed into being like a huge cross at an illuminated fête. Whether he went to the Palais de Justice, or to the Moulin-Rouge, he was greeted by the acclamations of the crowd, and princes begged for the honour of touching his hand.

And, in spite of all this, Raoul was not at peace. When in the little first-floor apartment hung with sky-blue draperies, intended by Madame de Bonmont to shelter their mutual love, he was always sombre and violent. When he heard his worth and praises shouted in the streets, when he could not listen to the rumbling wheels of an omnibus or the shriek of a tram without knowing that both vehicles contained the supporters and guardians of his honour, he still remained plunged in the bitterest, most dismal thoughts and cherished terrible designs. With frowning brows and clenched teeth he muttered curses ; he chewed threats as a sailor chews his tobacco. " Scoundrels ! Wretches ! I'll run them through the body ! " It may seem almost impossible, but is, nevertheless, true, that he was unconscious of the people's acclamations ; he did not hear them, and the only people he thought of were his few accusers, all of whom were believed to be dispersed, destroyed, and reduced to powder. In his imagination he saw them standing before him, with threatening faces, and at sight of them terror made his yellow eyes start from his head.

His fury was a source of consternation to poor Madame de Bonmont, who only heard hoarse cries of hatred and vengeance coming from the lips which should have given her kisses and words of love. And she was the more surprised and un-

comfortable because her lover's threats were
directed as much against friend as against foe. For
when he spoke of " running them through," Raoul
never stopped to make the subtle distinction between his defenders and his adversaries. His great
mind took in the whole of his country, yes, and the
whole of the human race.

e would spend hours every day pacing up and
down like a caged lion or panther in the two little
rooms that Madame de Bonmont had hung with blue
silk and furnished with cosy lounges in the hope of
better things. " I'll do for them ! " he muttered
as he strode up and down.

Seated in one corner of the big couch she would
follow his movements with a timid look, and listen
anxiously to his words ; not that the sentiments
expressed by him appeared to her in any way
unworthy of her beloved ; instinctively submissive,
naturally docile, she admired strength in all its
forms, and flattered herself with the vague hope
that a man who was capable of such wholesale
slaughter, might also, at another time, be capable of
wonderful embraces. And sitting at one end of the
couch, she waited with half-closed eyes and gently
heaving bosom for her Raoul's mood to change.

She waited in vain ! The vociferations continued
to make her start :

" I'll do for them ! "

Occasionally she would timidly try to appease his fury ; in a voice as full as her figure she would murmur :

" But they are doing you full justice, dearest— every one knows you to be a man of honour ! "

It may be true that the slender, dark-haired David succeeded in calming the fury of Saul with his shepherd's lute, the sound of which was thinner than a cricket's chirrup ; Elizabeth, less fortunate than he, vainly offered to Raoul the Nirvana of her sighs and the splendour of her pink and white self. Without daring to look at him, she ventured to say :

" I cannot understand you, *mon ami*. You have confounded your detractors, the General embraced you in the middle of the street the other day, and the ministers . . ."

She got no further ; he burst out :

" You mention those blackguards to me ! They are only trying to find some way of getting at me. They would like to see me a hundred feet under the ground. But they had better be careful ! I will devour them piecemeal ! "

Then he came back to his dear, familiar thought :

" I must do for them ! "

This was his dream :

" I should like to be in an immense marble hall full of people, and to lay about me with a big stick, to strike for days and nights, until the floor, the ceiling, and the walls were red with blood ! "

She vouchsafed no reply, but only looked in silence at her breast, where lay the little bunch of violets she had bought for him and dared not offer.

He gave her no more love. It was over and done with. The hardest-hearted man would have taken pity on the pretty, gentle creature who, with her voluptuous body and skin of milk and roses, resembled some big, warm flower in its beauty, neglected, abandoned, and left without care or culture.

She was suffering, and, being piously inclined, she sought a remedy in religion. Thinking that an interview with Abbé Guitrel would be of great service to Raoul, she resolved to bring the priest and her lover together.

CHAPTER XV

EFORE dressing, Philippe Dellion pulled aside the window-curtains, and, looking out into the light-spangled night, watched the carriage lamps passing to and fro in the busy street. For a moment or two the sight pleased him ; he had been in this room, separated from the outer world, for the space of two hours.

"What are you looking at, *mon petit ?*" asked Madame de Gromance, sitting up in the bed and arranging her tumbled hair. " Do strike a light, it is impossible to see a thing."

He lighted the candles that stood in little copper stands on either side of a gilded clock adorned with shepherds and shepherdesses. The gentle light reflected itself in the wardrobe and made the rosewood cornice glisten. Little rays flickering everywhere in the room, lit up the scattered garments and died gently away in the curtains' folds.

The room was an apartment in a highly respectable hotel, in a street near the Boulevard des Capucines. Madame de Gromance, in her

wisdom, had selected it, refusing to have anything to do with the less subtle arrangements
of Philippe, who had hired a little *rez-de-
chaussée*, in the lonely Avenue Kléber. It was her
opinion that a woman who wished to keep her
affairs to herself must see that they take place
in the very heart of Paris, in some respectable
hotel frequented by people of divers races and
tongues. She hardly ever spent more than two
consecutive months in Paris, but she frequently
met Philippe there, and in far greater security
than she could have done in the provinces.

As she sat on the edge of the bed, the soft light fell
upon her fair fluffy hair, the milk-white skin of her
sloping shoulders, and her pretty but somewhat
drooping breast.

" I am sure I shall be late again," she said.
" Tell me the time, *mon petit*, and don't make a
mistake. It's really important ! "

" Why do you always call me ' *mon petit* ' ? Ten
past six," he returned in a surly voice.

" Ten past six ? Are you quite sure ? I call
you ' *mon petit* ' because I love you. What would
you have me call you ? "

" I call you Clotilde, you might occasionally call
me Philippe."

" I never do call people by their names."

" Oh, well ! no matter ! " he said bitterly. " I

don't presume to imagine that I shall change your habits."

She picked up her stockings from the floor, stretching her back like a cat about to pounce upon a mouse.

" What does it matter ? I never think of calling you by your Christian name, as I do my husband, or my brother, or my cousins."

" All right ! all right ! " he replied. " I will conform to custom."

" What custom ? "

Jumping up with her stockings in her hand, she came across the room and kissed him upon the neck.

Though by no means a clever man, he was suspicious, and an idea that had lately struck him was worrying him ; he suspected that Madame de Gromance was careful to avoid making use of his name, or of the name of any other lover, for fear of getting mixed in a moment of supreme excitement, for she was a sensitive soul !

He was not exactly jealous, but he had a certain amount of proper pride. Had he known that Madame de Gromance was unfaithful to him, his vanity would have suffered. On the other hand, the desire he had for the pretty creature was proportionate only to the desire he believed her to inspire in others. He was not at all sure that it

was considered necessary to be the lover of Madame
de Gromance, or of any other society woman ;
many of his intimate friends preferred an automobile to a mistress. He liked her well enough,
and had no objection to being her lover so long
as it was considered the thing, but if it was not,
he could not see why he should persist in the
matter. The deep animal instinct in him and
his outlook as a man of the world scarcely
agreed, and he was not clever enough to conciliate
such conflicting elements, the result being that
there was an imperfect, indeterminate tone about
his remarks that rather fascinated Madame de Gromance, who would not take the trouble of finding
the solution and making things clear. If it came to
the point, his charmer would say to him, "Of course
I've never loved any man but you!" but that was less
in the hope of convincing him than in the desire
to say the thing most fitting the occasion. And
at such moments when reflection is at a disadvantage
the tremendous difficulty presented by belief in
such a statement never occurred to him. Later,
when he began to reason, doubt assailed him.

His doubt found expression in cruel and sarcastic
remarks, and he practised the art of keeping his
mind in a state of vague unrest. On this particular
occasion he was less sulky and bitter than usual,
and hardly even jealous or mistrustful. He merely

displayed the ill-humour that naturally follows gratified desire.

Madame de Gromance, on the contrary, was quite prepared for the blackest fit of spite and unkindness, for on that very day her strength, combined with her weakness, her natural inspiration and deep artifice had obtained from him a more liberal display of affection than that which on principle he usually vouchsafed. She had led him to overstep the bounds of moderation, a thing he did not easily forgive, for he was solicitous of his health, and keen on keeping in condition for exercise and sport. Whenever Madame de Gromance led him further than he wished, he afterwards avenged himself by unkind words and a still more unkind silence. She did not mind, for she loved love, and experience had taught her that all men are disagreeable as soon as they get what they want. So she calmly awaited the reproaches she knew she deserved. She was disappointed in her expectations, however, for a remark from Philippe showed her that his mind was quiet and at rest.

" My shirtmaker is an ass," he said.

He carefully dressed himself before the glass, and turned great thoughts over and over in his mind. After a few moments of silence he asked in quite a pleasant tone :

" You know Loyer, don't you ? "

Fresh-complexioned and slightly flushed with her
white figure thrown into relief by the dark velvet of
the arm-chair, she was sitting buttoning her boots.
As she sat there, with her head and neck bent over
her crossed legs, the light shone upon her hair and
upon the bare limbs revealed by the short garment
she wore, making one think of an allegorical figure
from some painted Venetian ceiling. This resemblance did not, however, strike Philippe. He repeated his question :

" Do you know Loyer ? "

She lifted her head, dangling the buttonhook from
the tips of her fingers.

" Loyer, the Cabinet Minister ? Yes, I know
him."

" Do you know him well ? "

" Not very well, but I do know him."

The man under discussion, Loyer the senator,
keeper of the seals and Minister of Public Worship,
was an insignificant-looking old bachelor, honest
enough outside politics, a bit of a lawyer, and a
philosopher, whose hair had turned grey in the
enjoyment of clandestine love and tavern nights.
As he had not made his entry into society until
somewhat late in life, the women he met there were
a continual source of wonder to him, as he de-
voured them with gold-spectacled eyes.

He was very young for his sixty years, and had

known how to appreciate Madame de Gromance at her true value when he had first met her in the drawing-rooms of the *préfecture*. That was seven years ago.

Loyer had come to the town of M. Worms-Clavelin to unveil a statue to Joan of Arc, and had then pronounced the memorable speech that terminated magnificently with a comparison between the Maid and Gambetta, each of whom was transfigured, said the orator, " by the sublime light of patriotism." The Conservatives, who already were secretly siding with the Radicals, because of their financial policy, were grateful to the minister for binding them anew to the old regime with the honourable bonds of a generous sentiment.

M. de Gromance had offered him his hand, saying: "'As an old Royalist, Monsieur le Ministre, I thank you for Jeanne and for France ! "

When Loyer walked that evening with Madame de Gromance in the gardens of the *préfecture*, lighted up by hundreds of Chinese lanterns, fixed to the trees — trees that had been planted in 1690 by the Benedictines of Sillé, so that two centuries later Madame Worms-Clavelin might enjoy their shade — the minister, who had been told by the Préfet himself that the "old Royalist" was the most deluded husband in the Department, whispered

a few gallantries into the young woman's pink ear.
He was a Burgundian, and prided himself on being
a daring one at that. Impressed by the beauty of
the historic evening, he remarked as he took leave of
Madame de Gromance that the illuminations made
him inclined to dream. Madame de Gromance liked
Loyer, and subsequently begged of him several
little favours on behalf of her parish and district,
which the old fellow granted, demanding nothing
in return, quite content with being allowed to
pat the arms and shoulders of the beautiful
ralliée and to ask in a jocular manner after her
" Old Royalist."

She could therefore quite well allow that she
knew Loyer, who was in the Radical Cabinet as
Minister of Public Worship.

"I know Loyer as one knows a person who does not
belong to the same set as oneself. Why do you ask ?"

" Because if you know him well enough, I want
you to ask him to do something for me."

" What ! Do you want to bear off the academic
honours like M. Bergeret ? "

" No," said Philippe seriously. " It is something
more important. I want you to speak to him
about Abbé Guitrel."

In her surprise she stood up, revealing a glimpse
of dazzling flesh above her stockings. Astonishment
gave her the semblance of innocence,

P

" Why ? " she demanded.

He was carefully knotting his tie.

" I want Loyer to make him bishop."

" Bishop ! "

The word produced abundant and definite ideas in the mind of Madame de Gromance.

For years and years she had seen the short, fat figure, mitre-crowned and covered with the gold-embroidered cope, rubicund, shapeless, dignified, of Monseigneur Charlot, officiating on fête-days at the cathedral. She had often dined with him, and had received him at her own table. In common with all the other ladies of the diocese, she admired the clever repartee and handsome red-stockinged calves of the cardinal-archbishop. She also knew a considerable number of bishops, all of whom were worthy men, but she had never reflected on the influences that confer episcopal dignity upon a priest. It seemed to her strange that a kind-hearted but common and coarse-minded man like Loyer should have the power to create a prelate like Monseigneur Charlot.

She sat there, thoughtful, looking around the room, from the tumbled bed to the little table, upon which were placed a bottle of sherry and some biscuits ; from the chair on which she had thrown some of her garments to the untidy dressing-table, her beautiful, unintelligent eyes wandered, seeing nothing but lace rochets, crosiers, crosses, and amethyst rings. Feeling absolutely at a loss, she inquired :

"Do you think bishops are made like that ? "

"Of course," he replied with assurance.

"And so you think, *mon petit*, that if I were to ask Loyer to make Abbé Guitrel a bishop——"

He assured her that Loyer, who was an old gallant, would not refuse that to a pretty woman.

She fixed her pink silk knickers to a hook on her silk stays. Then, as he pressed for a reply, and insisted upon her going immediately to see the minister, she grew exceedingly curious, and not a little suspicious.

"But, *mon petit*, why do you want Abbé Guitrel to be made a bishop ? Why ? "

"To please Mother. And because I like the fellow ; he is intelligent and up to date — there aren't so many like him. Yes, he really is advanced and in the Pope's good books besides. And Mother would be so delighted."

"Then why doesn't she go herself and settle the business with Loyer ? "

"In the first place, darling, it wouldn't be at all the same. Besides, my parents are not in very great favour with this Cabinet. My father, as President of the Chambre Syndicale des Métaux, has been protesting against the new tariffs. You cannot imagine how irritating these economic questions can be."

But she knew quite well that he was deceiving her, and that it was not filial love that made him dabble in ecclesiastical affairs.

She went round the room in her pink knickers of flowered silk, lithe, agile, and pliable, stooping here and there over the scattered garments, searching for her petticoat.

" *Mon petit*, I want your advice——"

" What about ? "

After spending an unconscionable time arranging his tie in front of the glass, and lighting a cigarette, he complacently sat watching her as she flitted about the room in a costume that exaggerated so prettily all that was feminine in her exceedingly feminine body. He did not know whether to think her graceful or ridiculous. He did not know whether he ought to think such things really unbeautiful, or whether he should experience some slight artistic pleasure in beholding them. His doubt arose from the recollection of a long discussion which had taken place the winter before in the smoking-room at his father's house, between two old gallants, M. de Terremondre, who could think of nothing more adorable than a pretty woman in her knickers and stays, and Paul Flin, who, on the contrary, pitied a woman for her ungraceful appearance at this

particular stage of her toilet. Philippe had followed
this entertaining discussion, and could not make
up his mind which of the two was right. Terremondre was a man of experience, but he was old-
fashioned and too artistic. Paul Flin was considered
less clever, but very smart. Philippe's natural
malevolence and elective affinities were making him
incline to the latter's theory when Madame de
Gromance put on her pink silk petticoat.

"*Mon petit,* do advise me. This year fur
dresses are all the rage, but what do you say to
a red cloth dress—a rich red, say ruby—a fur coat
and fur toque with a bunch of Parma violets ? "

He did not speak, and only betrayed his thought
by a nod of the head. At last he opened his mouth,
whence issued, instead of words, the smoke of his
cigarette.

Deep in her dream she continued :

"With buttons of old paste, very narrow sleeves
and a tight skirt."

He spoke at last :

"A tight skirt — yes, that would be all right."

Then she remembered that he knew nothing
about skirts or bodices. An idea flashed into her
mind and matured.

"It is funny !" she cried. "Only the men who
do not care about women are interested in women's
dress. And the men who like them never notice

what they wear. Now you, for instance. I am sure you could not tell me what dress I had on last Saturday at your mother's, while little Suequet, whose tastes, as everybody knows, are different, talks *lingerie* and *chiffons* quite prettily. He is a born dressmaker and milliner, that boy! Tell me, how do you account for it?"

"It would take too long."

"You are sitting on my skirt, *mon petit.* While I think of it, Emmanuel says that you are neglecting him. Yesterday he expected you to come and see a horse that he wants to buy, and you didn't turn up. He's awfully annoyed!"

At these words Philippe broke into a torrent of abuse.

"Your husband bores me to tears. He's a grotesque fool—and the most awful bore! You must admit yourself that pottering about all day in his stables, his kennels, and his kitchen garden —for he goes in for gardening too, the duffer —looking at the dogs' food, the horses, and such-like isn't what you might call exciting. And then when one comes to think of you and me, I must say it is a bit thick for your husband to hang on to me as he does. He's such a fool that he makes people talk. It's perfectly true, I tell you, people are beginning to talk."

She answered him gently and seriously while she slipped on her skirt.

"Don't abuse my husband, Philippe. As I am obliged to have a husband of some sort, it is a very good thing mine is like he is. Just think for a moment, *mon petit*, we might have somebody much worse to deal with."

Philippe's anger would not be calmed.

"And he loves you, the beast!"

She made a little grimace and shrugged her shoulders, as if to imply that that was not worth mentioning. That is how Philippe chose to interpret it, for he went on to enlarge upon the subject.

"As far as that goes, anyone can see at a glance that he's not much of a man with the women, but, even then, some things don't bear thinking about."

Madame de Gromance turned to Philippe a beautiful look full of happiness and peace, a look that counselled the banishment of all painful thoughts, and going up to him placed full upon his lips a kiss, magnificent as a royal scarlet seal.

"Mind my cigarette," he said.

By this time she was clothed in a very simple grey dress, and was arranging her toque upon her fluffy hair. Suddenly she broke into a laugh, and he inquired the cause of her amusement.

"Oh, nothing!"

Then, as he persisted in his inquiry:

"Well, I was only thinking that when your mother went to see her lover — years ago, you know — she must have found her hair a terrible nuisance, that is if she wore it as it is in that portrait you have of her at home."

He made no reply, not quite knowing how to treat a joke of this description, which inwardly shocked him.

" You're not angry, surely," she went on. " You do love me, don't you ? "

No, he was not angry ; yes, he loved her ; and she returned to her original idea.

" It is strange, you know. Sons always believe in the virtue of their mothers ; daughters, too, but not so implicitly. And yet the fact of a woman having had children is surely not sufficient to prove that she has never had lovers."

She reflected a moment, and then went on:

" Things are complicated in this world. Good-bye, *mon petit*. I am walking, and have only just time to get there."

" Why are you walking ? "

" Because it is good for my health, and then it explains my not having the carriage. And it's rather fun."

She scrutinized herself in the looking-glass, first three-quarter-ways, then sideways, finally glancing at her back view.

" At this hour of the day, for instance, I am sure to collect a good number of followers."

" Why ? "

" Because I look rather nice."

" What I mean is, why at this hour specially ? "

" Because it is evening. The streets are always full just before dinner-time."

" But who follows you ? What sort of people ? "

" All sorts. Men about town, workmen and priests. Yesterday a nigger followed me. He had on a hat that shone like a mirror. He was awfully sweet."

" Did he speak to you ? "

" Oh, yes. He said : ' Madame, will you go for a drive with me ? Or are you afraid of losing your reputation ? ' "

" What a silly remark ! "

" Some of them say much sillier things," she answered gravely. " Adieu, *mon petit*, we've had a lovely time to-day."

Her hand was already on the key of the door when he stopped her.

" Clotilde," said he, " promise me you will go and see Loyer, and that you will say to him very nicely, ' M. Loyer, you have a vacant see to dispose of. Make Abbé Guitrel bishop, you cannot do better. The Pope thinks very highly of him.' "

She shook her pretty head.

" Go and see Loyer for that ? Can you imagine

me in the cage of that old gorilla ? We must make some special arrangement, meet him at some friend's house, or something of the sort."

" But," objected Philippe, " it's very important. At any moment Loyer may sign the appointments now. There are several vacant sees."

She reflected a moment, and, making a special effort to think clearly, said :

" You must be mistaken, *mon petit,*" said she. " It's *not* Loyer who appoints the bishops. It's the Pope, really it is, or the Nuncio. I can prove that, for the other day Emmanuel said, ' The Nuncio ought to overcome the modesty of M. de Goulet, and offer him a bishopric.' So you see."

He tried to convince her to the contrary, taking the trouble to explain the reason why.

" Listen to me ! The minister chooses the bishops, and the Nuncio confirms the minister's choice. That is what is called the Concordat. You must say to Loyer : ' I know of an intelligent liberal-minded priest, one that the Pope thinks of very highly '——"

" Yes, yes, I know ! " She opened wide eyes of wonder. "It's an extraordinary thing you are asking of me, *mon petit !* "

Her amazement came from the fact that she was religious, and had the greatest veneration for holy things. He was a little less religious than she, but perhaps a trifle more scrupulous, and in his innermost self he recognized that she was right, and that it was an extraordinary thing to ask of her. But he was so anxious for the matter to be concluded that he hastened to reassure her.

" I am not asking you to do anything forbidden by religion," he protested.

In the meanwhile her first curiosity had returned.

" But why do you want M. Guitrel to be chosen, *mon petit ?* " she asked.

He answered confusedly, as he had done before :

" Mother would be pleased, and other people too."

" What other people ? "

" Oh, heaps of them — the Bonmonts."

" The Bonmonts ? But they are Jews ! "

" That doesn't matter ; there are Jews even among the clergy."

Madame de Gromance grew more suspicious as soon as she learned that the Bonmonts were mixed up in the singular affair, but being affectionate and easily led she promised Philippe she would do as he asked.

CHAPTER XVI

L'ABBÉ GUITREL, candidate for the episcopacy, was ushered into the study of the Nuncio, Monseigneur Cima, whose appearance at first sight came as a surprise, for his pale, large-featured countenance, on which the years had left traces of fatigue, showed no signs of age. At forty, he looked rather like a sickly youth, and when he cast down his eyes his face was as the face of a dead man. He signed to the visitor to be seated, and, assuming his usual attitude, leaned back in his easy chair, and prepared to listen to him. With his right elbow in his left hand, and his head resting in the hollow of his right hand, he had a grace that struck one as vaguely funereal, and called to mind certain figures on ancient bas-reliefs. When in repose his face was veiled in melancholy, but as soon as he smiled it radiated humour. The gaze of his beautiful dark eyes gave one a feeling of discomfort; at Naples he was said to possess the evil eye; in France he passed for a clever politician.

M. l'Abbé Guitrel thought it advisable to

make only a passing allusion to the object of his
visit.

Mother Church in her wisdom might dispose
of him as she judged good. All his feelings of love
for her were blended in an entire obedience to her
will !

" Monseigneur," he added, " I am a priest, in
other words a soldier, and I aspire to the glory of
obedience ! "

Slowly bending his head, as a sign of approbation,
Monseigneur Cima asked the Abbé if he had been
in any way acquainted with M. Duclou, the late
Bishop of Tourcoing.

" I knew him when he was Curé at Orleans,
Monseigneur."

" Orleans ?   A pleasant town, I have relations
there, distant cousins of mine. M. Duclou was
very old when he died. Do you know what caused
his death ? "

" Stone, Monseigneur."

" The cause of the death of many old men,
although science has discovered many things to
mitigate this terrible malady."

" Yes, indeed, Monseigneur ! "

" I used to know M. Duclou at Rome ; he often
had a rubber of whist with me. Have you ever
been to Rome, M. Guitrel ? "

" Monseigneur, that is a joy so far denied me,

but I have long sojourned there in thought. My spirit has outstripped my body in its journey to the Vatican."

"Yes, yes; the Pope would be very pleased to see you. He likes France very much. The best time for a visit to Rome is during the spring, for in summer malaria is rife in the countryside, and in some parts of the city even."

"I do not fear malaria."

"Of course not. Besides, provided one takes certain precautions, one can always ward off fevers; you must never go out at night without your cloak, and foreigners especially should never go out in open vehicles after the sun has set."

"I have heard, Monseigneur, that the Coliseum by moonlight is a truly wonderful sight."

"The air is treacherous in that district, and the gardens of the Villa Borghese are also to be avoided for the same reason."

"Really, Monseigneur?"

"Yes, yes! I, who am Roman-born, cannot endure the climate of Rome. I prefer to go to Brussels. I was there for a year some time ago, and can think of no town that I like better. I have relations there. Tourcoing, is that a large town?"

"About 40,000 inhabitants, I believe, Monseigneur. It is a manufacturing town."

"I know! I know! M. Duclou used to tell

me in Rome that he could only find one fault
with his flock : they drank beer. He used to say
that if they would only drink the light wines of
Orleans they would be the most perfect Christians
in the world, but hops made them melancholy."

" M. Duclou was a very witty man."

" He disliked beer, and once I surprised him
very much by telling him that it was quite popular
in Italy nowadays. There are very prosperous
German beer-houses in Florence, Rome, Naples,
and most of the other towns. Do you like beer,
M. Guitrel ? "

" I do not dislike it, Monseigneur."

The Nuncio gave his ring to the priest, who kissed
it and took a respectful leave.

The Nuncio rang the bell.

" Show M. Lantaigne in."

Having kissed the ring, the director of the Grand
Séminaire was invited to sit down and state his
business.

He said :

" Monseigneur, I have sacrificed to the Pope and
to necessity all the ties that bound me to the Royal
House of France ; I have trampled down the
dearest hopes of my heart, which was only what I
owed to the Father of the Faithful and the unity
of the Church. If His Holiness raises me to the
see of Tourcoing, I will rule it in his interest and

in the interest of France. A bishop is a ruling power, and I can answer for my steadfastness and devotion."

Slowly bending his head as a sign of approbation, Monseigneur Cima asked Abbé Lantaigne whether he had been in any way acquainted with M. Duclou, the late Bishop of Tourcoing.

" I only knew him slightly," replied M. Lantaigne, " and long before his elevation to the bishopric. I remember having lent him some of my sermons when I had more of them than I knew what to do with."

" He was not young when we lost him. Do you know what caused his death ? "

" I do not know."

" I knew M. Duclou in Rome ; he often used to play a rubber of whist with me. Have you ever been to Rome, M. Lantaigne ? "

" Never, Monseigneur."

" You should go. The Pope would be very pleased to see you ; he likes France very much. But you must be careful when you go ; the climate of Rome is bad for foreigners. During the summer malaria is rife in the countryside, and even in some parts of the city. The best season to visit Rome is the spring. I was born in Rome, of Roman parents, and I much prefer Paris or Brussels. Brussels is a very pleasant town. I have relations there. Tell me, Tourcoing, is it a very large town ? "

" It is one of the oldest sees of Northern France, Monseigneur, and is notorious for its long line of saintly bishops, from the blessed St. Loup to Monseigneur de la Thrumellière, the immediate predecessor of M. Duclou."

" Tell me, what are the people of Tourcoing like ? "

" They are good Church people, Monseigneur, and tend more to the Belgian form of Catholicism than to the French."

" Yes, yes, I know. M. Duclou, the late lamented Bishop of Tourcoing, told me one day in Rome that he had only one fault to find with his flock : they drank beer. He used to say that if they would only drink the light wines of Orleans, they would be the most perfect Christians in the world, but the juice of the hop filled them with its melancholy and bitterness."

" Monseigneur, allow me to say one thing : Monseigneur Duclou was both weak and brainless. He never brought out the energetic qualities of the sturdy northerners under his care. He was not a bad man, but his dislike of evil was only moderate. The Catholic town of Tourcoing must shine out on the whole of the Catholic world. Should His Holiness judge me worthy to fill the seat of the blessed St. Loup, I swear in ten years' time to have won all hearts by the sacred energy of good works ;

Q

to have stolen back all the souls gone over to the enemy and to re-establish around me the oneness of belief. In the depths of her innermost soul, France is Christian, and only needs energetic leaders. The Church is dying from sheer inanition."

Monseigneur Cima rose from his chair, and held out to Abbé Lantaigne his golden ring, saying:

"You must go to Rome, M. l'Abbé, you must go to Rome!"

CHAPTER XVII

THE drawing-room of the house in the grey Batignolles quarter was humble, the only decorations being copies of the engravings in the Louvre, little statues, cups and dishes of Sèvres china, trivial-looking ornaments, which somehow proclaimed the fact that the lady of the house was connected with Government officials.

Madame Cheiral, *née* Loyer, was the sister of the Minister of Justice and Public Worship. She was the widow of a commission-agent in the Rue d'Hauteville, who had died without leaving a penny, and she had attached herself to her brother, partly for the sake of a home, and partly out of maternal ambition. She ruled the old bachelor, who ruled the country, and had forced him to take as his secretary-in-chief her son Maurice, who was not fitted for anything in particular, and was good for nothing except some public office.

Uncle Loyer had a room in the little flat of the

Avenue de Clichy, where he came to stay for a while every spring, at which season he was subject to attacks of giddiness and drowsiness, for he was getting old. As soon, however, as his head felt better and his tread became more assured, he returned to the attic-room, where he had lived for half a century, a room where he had twice been arrested by the agents of the Empire, and from which he could see the trees of the Luxembourg. He still kept the pipe of Jules Grévy in this garret of his.

This pipe was perhaps the most treasured possession of the old fellow, who had gone through many phases as a Member of Parliament: the days of eloquence and the days of affairs. He had controlled as Minister of the Interior the secret funds of three budgets. He had bought many a conscience for his party, a corrupter of others, but incorruptible himself. He had always had an infinite indulgence for the hypocrisies of his friends, but was jealous himself of retaining in the midst of his power the vantage-ground of a simulated poverty that was at once cynical, obstinate, deep-rooted, and honourable.

His eye was dim now and his mind inactive, but in the intervals, when his old skill and decisive spirit returned to him, he applied all his remaining vigour to concentrated thought, and the game of billiards.

Madame Cheiral, whose intelligence was limited and whose skill but moderate, did what she liked with the cunning, quiet, silent, and coarse-minded old man, who for the sixth time in his career had been selected as a member of the cabinet that had followed upon the heels of the clerical cabinet, and who saw his nephew fulfilling the indefinite duties of secretary-in-chief without an idea of leadership, nor a glimmer of moral principle. No doubt, Loyer was somewhat surprised to find that his nephew had reactionary and clerical tendencies, but he was too much inclined to apoplexy to run the risk of thwarting his sister.

Madame Cheiral was staying at home that day, and when Madame Worms-Clavelin called to see her somewhat late in the afternoon, when no further callers were expected, she received her very cordially. They wished each other good-bye, for the *préfet's* wife was returning home on the morrow.

" Going already, darling ? "

" I must," replied Madame Worms-Clavelin sweetly, looking quite innocent in her black feather-trimmed hat.

She always affected this hat when paying calls, likening herself to a plume-bedecked horse attached to a funeral car.

" You must stay and dine with us, dear ; we so seldom see you in Paris. We shall be quite alone.

I don't think my brother will be here. He is so busy and engrossed in his work just now! But perhaps Maurice will be with us; the young men of to-day are much steadier than they used to be. Maurice often spends an evening at home with me."

She began to try to prevail upon Madame Worms-Clavelin with all the persuasive eloquence of a sociable soul.

"We shall be quite among ourselves. Your dress will do very nicely. I assure you we shall be absolutely *en famille*."

Now Madame Worms-Clavelin had obtained from the Minister of the Interior the Cross of the Legion of Honour for her husband; she had exacted from the Minister of Instruction and Public Worship a promise that the name of M. Guitrel, as candidate for the bishopric of Tourcoing, should be on the list of candidates selected for the six vacant sees, so there was nothing to keep her any longer in Paris. She had intended to return home that very evening.

She excused herself, saying that she had "so many things to see to," but Madame Cheiral insisted; then, as Madame Worms-Clavelin persisted in her refusal, she showed her displeasure by tightened lips and acid tones, so Madame Worms-Clavelin, who had no wish to annoy her, gave in.

" That's right ; and, as I said before, we shall be quite by ourselves."

They were by themselves, for Loyer never came, and Maurice, who was expected, did not turn up either. But in their place came a lady tobacconist* and a well-known elementary school teacher. The conversation was deep and serious. Madame Cheiral, who really was only interested in her own affairs, and who had no spite against anyone except her dearest friends, picked out the men whom she thought worthy of the Senate, the Chamber, and the Institute, not that she cared about politics, science, or literature, but because she thought it her duty, as the sister of a Cabinet Minister, to hold opinions on everything that contributed to the moral and intellectual greatness of her country.

Madame Worms-Clavelin listened to her with charming deference, always retaining the same air of innocence that she reserved for people who bored her. When in society she had a way of looking down which gave old gentlemen a thrill, and which to-day excited the admiration of the hoary-headed instructor of grammar and gymnastics, who endeavoured to press her foot with his own

---

* The sale of tobacco in France is controlled by the State, and given to the widows and daughters of Government officials, military and naval officers, etc.

under the table. However, she had made up her mind to return by train from the Avenue de Clichy to the Arc-de-Triomphe, where, among the radiating avenues that look like an enormous cross of honour, her boarding house was situated. But when she returned to the drawing-room on the arm of the old gentleman who had rendered such signal services to elementary instruction she found Maurice Cheiral, who had been detained at the ministry, and who, after dining at a restaurant, had returned home to dress, prior to spending the evening at a theatre.

He examined Madame Worms-Clavelin with interest, and sat down beside her on the comfortable old couch that stood under a great Sèvres dish decorated in neo-Chinese style, and suspended on the wall in a blue plush frame.

"Madame Clavelin! You are the very person I wanted to see!"

In her younger days Madame Worms-Clavelin had been thin and dark, and in such guise had not been unattractive to men. As time went on she became fat and fair, and in this guise she was again not unattractive to men.

"Did you see my uncle yesterday?"

"Yes. He was so sweet to me. How is he to-day?"

"Tired, very tired. He gave me the papers."

" What papers ? "

" The papers referring to the candidatures for
the six vacant sees. You are very anxious for Abbé
Guitrel to be elected, are you not ? "

" My husband is anxious. Your uncle told me
that the thing was settled."

" My uncle; you should not take any notice of
what he says — he is a Minister and cannot know.
People are always fooling him, and then he often says
what he does not mean. Why didn't you come to
me ? "

With charming modesty Madame Worms-Clavelin replied in a low voice:

" Well, I do come to you ! "

" And you are wise to do so," replied the secretary-
in-chief. " All the more so because the business is
not going on as you wish, and it depends upon me
whether it proceeds or not. My uncle told you, no
doubt, that he was going to present the six applica-
tions to the Pope ? "

" Yes."

" Well, they have already been presented. I
know that, for I sent them. I take a special interest
in Church matters. My uncle is one of the old
school; he does not understand the importance
of religion, while I realize it thoroughly. Now
this is how things stand : the six candidates have
been presented to the Pope, and the Holy Father

has only accepted four. As far as the other two are concerned, that is M. Guitrel and M. Morrue, he does not absolutely reject them, but he says he has not yet sufficient information concerning them." Maurice Cheiral shook his head gravely. "He has not sufficient information! And when he gets more I do not know what he will say. Between ourselves, dear lady, Guitrel looks to me a bit of a rogue, and we cannot be too careful in choosing our bishops. The clergy is a force upon which a prudent Government should be able to rely; we are just beginning to realize that."

"You are quite right," said Madame Clavelin.

"On the other hand," went on the secretary-in-chief, "your candidate seems learned, well read, and open-minded."

"Well?" asked Madame Worms-Clavelin, with a delightful smile.

"It is difficult!" replied Cheiral.

Cheiral was not a very clever man. He took few things into consideration, and always acted on reasons so futile that they were difficult to unravel. And so it was thought, that, being still young, he was swayed by personal motives. At the present time he had just finished reading a book by M. Imbert de Saint-Amand on the Tuileries during the second Empire; the splendour of the brilliant court had particularly taken his fancy, and the book had fired him with the desire to live, like the Duc de Morny, a life in which politics should be combined with pleasure and power of every description. He looked at Madame Worms-Clavelin in a manner the significance of which she thoroughly comprehended as she sat there silent with lowered gaze.

" My uncle," went on Cheiral, " gives me a free hand in this matter, which does not interest him at all. I can set about it in two ways. I can propose without further delay the four candidates accepted by the Holy Father, or I can tell the Nuncio that things will remain at a standstill until the Holy See has approved of six candidates. I have not yet made up my mind, but should be delighted to talk the matter over with you. Shall I expect you to-morrow afternoon at five o'clock, and wait for you in a closed carriage at the end of the Rue Vigny by the gates of the Park Monceau ? "

" There's not much risk in that," thought Madame Worms-Clavelin, her only reply a slight quivering of her downcast lids.

CHAPTER XVIII

ADAME DE BONMONT had no difficulty in bringing Raoul Marcien and M. l'Abbé Guitrel together at her house. The meeting was all that could be desired, for on his part M. l'Abbé Guitrel was full of unction, and Raoul, being a society man, knew what was due to the Church.

"Monsieur l'Abbé," he said, "I come of a family of priests and soldiers. I have been a soldier myself, and that means——"

He did not finish his sentence, for M. Guitrel held out his hand with a smile, saying:

"We may call it the alliance of the sword and the aspersorium." Then immediately resuming his priestly gravity: "And that is the most natural and the best of all alliances. We priests are soldiers too, and as far as I am concerned I am very fond of the army."

Madame de Bonmont gazed with sympathetic eyes at the Abbé, who continued:

" In the diocese to which I belong we have started clubs, where the soldiers can read good books as they smoke their cigars. The work is under the patronage of Monseigneur Charlot, and is both flourishing and useful. Let us not be unjust toward the age in which we live; if it contains much evil it also holds much that is good. We are engaged in a great fight, and that is, perhaps, to be preferred to the lukewarm state of those whom a great Christian poet has described as being shut out from both Heaven and Hell."

Raoul approved of this speech, but ventured no reply. He did not answer, by virtue of the fact that he had few ideas upon the subject, and also because his whole mind was absorbed in the thought of the three charges of cheating brought against him during the past week, which made it impossible for him to follow any abstract or general train of ideas.

Madame de Bonmont but dimly divined the real reason of his silence, and M. Guitrel did not understand it at all. With an honest desire to do the right thing, and keep the ball of conversation going, he asked M. Marcien if he knew Colonel Gandouin.

" He is an excellent man in every way," added the priest. " A fine example of the Christian and the soldier. He is respected by every right-thinking man in our diocese."

" Do I know Colonel Gandouin ! " cried Raoul.
" I know him only too well. I've had enough of
him ! I can't bear the man ! "

This outburst grieved Madame de Bonmont and
startled M. Guitrel. Neither of them knew that
four years before Colonel Gandouin, with six
other officers, had ordered Captain Marcien to
be placed on half-pay for habitual dereliction of
duty, that offence, selected from many others,
being the reason assigned.

From this moment the gentle Elizabeth gave
up hoping that any good would come of the interview which she had arranged to calm her Raoul,
to turn him away from thoughts of violence and
bring him back to thoughts of love. She opened
her heart, however, and in a tearful voice said to
the Abbé:

" Don't you think, M. l'Abbé, that when a
man is young and has a fine future before him, he
ought not to give way to discouragement and depression ? Ought he not, on the contrary, to avoid
all sad thoughts ? "

" Certainly, Madame la Baronne, certainly," replied M. l'Abbé Guitrel. " We must never give
way to discouragement, or abandon ourselves to
grief without cause. A good Christian never en-
courages gloomy thoughts, Madame la Baronne,
that is quite certain."

" Do you hear, M. Marcien ? " asked Madame de Bonmont.

But Raoul did not hear, and so the conversation dropped. Then Madame de Bonmont, being a kind-hearted woman, and anxious in the midst of her own worries to give a little pleasure to M. Guitrel, turned the topic of conversation.

" And so, M. l'Abbé," she said, " your favourite stone is the amethyst."

Guessing the drift of her remark, the priest answered severely and even harshly :

" Do not speak of that, Madame, I beg. Do not speak of that ! "

CHAPTER XIX

AVING risen early one morning, M. Bergeret, Professor of Latin literature, went for a walk into the country with Riquet. The two loved each other dearly, and were nearly always together. They had the same tastes, and both preferred a quiet, uneventful, and simple life.

Riquet's eyes always followed his master closely on these walks. He was afraid to let him out of his sight one instant, because he was not very sharp-scented, and, had he lost his master, could not have tracked him again. His beautiful, loving look was very engaging as he trotted by the side of M. Bergeret with an important air quite pretty to see. The Professor of Latin literature walked slowly or quickly according to the trend of his capricious fancy.

As soon as Riquet was a stone's throw ahead of his master, he turned round and waited for him with his nose in the air, and one of his front paws

lifted in an attitude of attention and watchfulness.
It did not take much to amuse either of them.
Riquet plunged into gardens and shops alike,
coming out again as hastily as he had entered.
On this particular day he bounded into the coal-
seller's office, to find himself confronted by a
huge snow-white pigeon that flapped its wings in
the darkness, to his extreme terror.

He came as usual to relate his adventure, with
eyes and paws and tail, to M. Bergeret, who said
jokingly :

" Yes, indeed, my poor Riquet, we have had a
terrible encounter, and have escaped the claws and
beak of a winged monster. That pigeon was an
awe-inspiring creature ! "

And M. Bergeret smiled. Riquet knew that
smile, and knew that his master was making fun of
him. This was a thing he could not bear. He
stopped wagging his tail, and walked with hanging
head, hunched-up back, and legs wide apart, as a
sign of annoyance.

" My poor Riquet," said M. Bergeret to him
again, " that bird, which your ancestors would
have eaten alive, alarms you. You are not hungry,
as they would have been, and you are not as brave
as they were ; the refinement of culture has made
a coward of you. It is questionable whether
civilization does not tend to make men less

R

courageous as well as less fierce. But civilized man, out of respect for his species, affects courage and makes of it an artificial virtue far more beautiful than the natural one. While, as for you, you shamelessly display your fear."

Riquet's annoyance, to tell the truth, was but slight, and only lasted a few minutes. All was forgiven and forgotten when the man and the dog entered the Josde woods just at the hour when the grass is wet with dew and light mists rise from the hills.

M. Bergeret loved the woods, and at sight of a blade of grass would lose himself in boundless reveries. Riquet, too, loved the woods. As he sniffed at the dead leaves his soul was filled with strange delight. In deep meditation, therefore, they followed the pathway leading to the Carrefour des Demoiselles, when they met a horseman returning to the town. It was M. de Terremondre, the county councillor.

" Good day, M. Bergeret," he cried, reining in his horse. " Well! Have you thought over my arguments of yesterday ? "

He had explained the evening before at Paillot's the reason why he was against the Jews.

When in the country, especially during the hunting season, M. de Terremondre's proclivities were anti-Jewish. When in Paris he dined with

rich Jews, whom he tolerated to the extent of in-
ducing them to buy pictures at a profit to himself.
At County Council meetings, with due consideration to the feelings that were paramount in his
county town, he was a Nationalist and an Anti-
Semite. But as there were no Jews in that town
the anti-Jewish crusade consisted principally in
attacks upon the Protestants, who formed a small,
austere, and exclusive community of their
own.

"So we are enemies," went on M. de Terremondre. "I am sorry for that, because you are a
clever man, but you live quite outside the social
movement, and are not mixed up in public life.
If you did as I do, and entered into it, your sym-
pathies would be anti-Jewish."

"You flatter me," said M. Bergeret. "The
Jewish race which peopled Chaldea, Assyria, and
Phœnicia in former times, and which founded cities
all along the Mediterranean coast, is composed to-
day of Jews scattered the world over, and also of
the countless Arab populations of Asia and Africa.
My heart is not great enough to contain so many
hatreds. Old Cadmus was a Jew, but I really
couldn't be the enemy of old Cadmus ! "

"You are joking," replied M. de Terremondre,
holding in his horse, who was nibbling at the
bushes. "You know as well as I do that the

anti-Jewish movement is directed solely against the Jews who have settled in France."

"Therefore I must hate 80,000 persons," said M. Bergeret. "That is still too many; I have not the strength for it!"

"No one asks you to hate them," said M. de Terremondre. "But Jews and Frenchmen cannot live together. The antagonism is ineradicable, it is in the blood."

"I believe, on the contrary," said M. Bergeret, "that the Jews are particularly assimilable, and have the most plastic and malleable natures in the world. With the same readiness that the niece of Mardocheus entered the harem of Ahasuerus in bygone days, so the daughters of our Jewish financiers marry nowadays the heirs to the greatest names in Christian France. After marriages such as these it is rather late in the day to speak of incompatibility of race. Then, I think it a bad thing to make a distinction of race in any country; it is not the race that makes the nation, and there is not a single country in Europe that has not been founded on a multitude of mixed and different races. When Caesar entered Gaul it was peopled by Celts, Gauls, Iberians, all differing in origin and religion. The tribes that set up the cromlechs were not of the same blood as those who honoured bards and druids. Into this human mixture the different invasions poured Germans, Romans, Saracens, and out of the whole a nation arose, the brave and lovable people of France, who, not so very long ago, were the teachers of justice, liberty, and philosophy to the entire world. Think of the beautiful words of Renan; I wish I could remember them exactly: 'What makes a nation is the memory of the great things its people have done together, and the will they have to accomplish others.'"

"Excellent!" said M. de Terremondre. "But as I have not the will to accomplish great things with the Jews, I remain an Anti-Semite."

"Are you quite sure that it is possible for your feelings to be wholly anti-Jewish?" asked M. Bergeret.

"I do not understand you," replied M. de Terremondre.

"Then I will explain myself," said M. Bergeret. "There is one fact that never varies: each time there is an attack on the Jews, a goodly number of them side with the enemy. That is just what happened to Titus."

At this point in the conversation Riquet sat down in the middle of the road and looked resignedly at his master.

"You will agree," went on M. Bergeret, " that between the years 67 and 70 A.D. Titus was a strong

Anti-Semite.   He took Jotapate, and exterminated
its inhabitants.   He conquered Jerusalem, burned
the Temple, and reduced to ashes and ruins the
city which afterwards received the name of Œlia
Capitolina.   The seven-branched candlestick was
carried in his triumphal procession to Rome, and,
I think, without doing you an injustice, I may say
that that was Anti-Semitism carried to a degree
which you people can never hope to attain.   Well !
Titus, the destroyer of Jerusalem, had many
friends among the Jews.   Berenice was deeply
attached to him, and you know as well as I do that
it was against his will and against hers that he left
her.   Flavius Josephus was his friend, and Flavius
was not one of the least of his nation.   He was
descended from the Asmonean kings, lived the
life of a strict Pharisee, and wrote Greek correctly
enough.   After the demolition of the temple and
holy city he followed Titus to Rome, and became
the intimate friend of the Emperor.   He received
the freedom of the city, the title of Roman Knight,
and a pension.   And do not imagine, monsieur,
that in so doing he was betraying his race.   On the
contrary, he remained faithful to the law, and
applied himself to the collection of national
antiquities.   In short, he was a good Jew in his
own way and a friend of Titus.   Now there have
always been men like Flavius in Israel.   As you

pointed out, I live a secluded life and know nothing
of what goes on in the world, but it would be a
great surprise to me if at the present crisis the
Jews were not divided amongst themselves, and
if a great number of them were not on your
side."

"Some of them are with us, as you say," replied
M. de Terremondre. "All the more credit to
them."

"I thought as much," said M. Bergeret. "And,
what is more, I am sure that there are some clever
ones among them who will make their mark in
this crusade against themselves. About thirty
years ago a senator, a very clever man, who admired
the Jewish faculty for getting on, and who cited as
an example a certain court chaplain of Jewish
origin, used the following words, which have since
been much quoted. ' See,' said he, ' here is a Jew
who has gone into the Church, and now he is a
Monseigneur. Let us not revive the prejudices of
barbaric times. Let us not ask if a man is a Jew
or Christian, but only if he is an honest man and
capable of serving his country.' "

M. de Terremondre's horse began to plunge,
and Riquet, coming up to his master, begged him,
with gentle, loving look, to continue the interrupted
walk.

"Do not run away with the idea," went on

M. de Terremondre, "that I include all Jews in
the same blind feeling of dislike. I have many
excellent friends among them, but my love for my
country makes an Anti-Semite of me."

He held out his hand to M. Bergeret, and turned
his horse around. He was quietly proceeding on
his way when the professor called him back.

"Hi! A word in your ear, dear M. de Terremondre. Now that the die is cast, and that you
and your friends have quarrelled with the Jews,
be very careful that you owe them nothing, and
give them back the God you have taken from them
—for you have taken their God."

"Jehovah?" asked M. de Terremondre.

"Yes, Jehovah! If I were in your place, I would
beware of Him. He was a Jew at heart, and who
knows whether He has not always remained a Jew?
Who knows whether at this moment He is not
avenging His people? All that we have seen
lately, the confessions that burst forth like thunder-
claps, the plain speaking, the revelations proceeding
from all parts, the assembly of red-robed judges
which you were not able to hinder even when you
seemed all-powerful, who can tell whether Jehovah
has not dealt these crushing blows? They savour
of His old biblical style, and I seem to recognize His
handiwork."

M. de Terremondre's horse was already disappearing behind the bushes round the bend of the path, and Riquet trotted along contentedly through the grass.

" Beware ! " repeated M. Bergeret. " Do not keep their God." .

CHAPTER XX

ADAME WORMS - CLAVELIN came along through the rainy darkness, holding up her umbrella, and walking with the brisk, decided step which, for a wonder, had not grown heavy from long years spent in provincial towns. The door of the carriage that was waiting for her in front of the gates of the Park Monceau, opened a little, and then stood wide, and Madame Worms-Clavelin slipped calmly in and took a seat beside the young secretary, who immediately inquired as to her health.

" I am always well," she replied, adding, " What awful weather ! "

Streams of rain were running down the carriage windows ; the street noises were drowned in the damp air, and all that could be heard was the gentle drip of the raindrops.

When the carriage began to roll with a muffled sound over the paved road, she asked :

" Where are we going ? "

" Where you like."

" I don't mind—Neuilly way, I should think."

Having given instructions to the driver, Maurice Cheiral turned to the *préfet's* wife and said:

" I have much pleasure in informing you that the appointment of Abbé Guitrel (Joachim) to the See of Tourcoing will be announced in to-morrow's *Officiel.* I do not want to boast, but I can assure you that it has not been a very easy matter to arrange. The Nuncio is great at procrastination. People of that description make use of a prodigious amount of inactivity—Well, anyhow, everything is settled."

" That's good," replied Madame Worms-Clavelin. " I am sure you have rendered a service to the progressive republican party, and that the Moderates will have every reason to be pleased with their new bishop."

" At any rate," went on Maurice Cheiral, " you are satisfied."

After a long silence he continued:

" Just think, I never slept all night. I was thinking of you, and longing to see you again."

The strange thing was that he was speaking the truth, and that the expectation of this rendezvous had excited him. But he spoke in a joking tone and drawling voice that made his words appear false, besides which he was wanting both in assurance and decision.

Madame Worms-Clavelin quite thought she would leave the carriage as she had entered it. Assuming a serious and gentle expression, she said in a sympathetic tone :

" Thank you, dear M. Cheiral. Put me down here, if you please, and remember me to your mother."

And she held out her hand, a little, stumpy hand clad in an exceedingly dirty glove. But he held it tightly, becoming tender and insistent, full of desire and amour-propre.

" I am as muddy as a water spaniel," she remarked, just as he was about to find that out for himself.

While he adhered to his resolve, in spite of the obstacles of circumstances and environment, she showed the most perfect good taste and simplicity. With wonderful tact, she avoided all the unpleasantness arising from an over-prolonged resistance or a too rapid resignation. In like manner she avoided any remark that might reveal either ironical indifference or interested participation. She behaved perfectly. She had no feeling of dislike for the young statesman, who was so innocent at the very moment when he believed himself to be so wicked, and feelings of real regret came over her as she reflected that she might have been more careful in selecting her *lingerie* for the occasion; she never had been careful enough of that, but of late years her carelessness had become somewhat excessive. Her greatest merit on this occasion was in keeping clear of all emphasis and exaggeration.

After a while, Maurice suddenly became quiet, indifferent, even a trifle bored. He talked of things quite foreign to their present situation, and peered through the blurred window-panes at the streets that looked as though the carriage were going along at the bottom of an aquarium ; all that could be seen through the rain was the gas-jets, and here and there the glass jars in the windows of the chemists' shops.

" What awful rain ! " sighed Madame Worms-Clavelin.

" The weather has been dreadful for the last week," said Maurice Cheiral, " simply rotten. Is it the same in your part of the country ? "

" We get more rain in our department than in any other in France," replied Madame Worms-Clavelin with charming sweetness. " But there is never any mud on the broad, gravelled garden paths of the Préfecture. Then we country people wear clogs."

" Do you know," said Cheiral, " that I have never been to your town ? "

" There are beautiful walks there," replied Madame Worms-Clavelin, " and the surroundings are charming. Do come and see us. My husband would be delighted."

" Does your husband like living there ? "

" Yes, he likes it because he has been successful there."

In her turn, she tried to see through the clouded panes and to pierce the thick darkness that was full of fugitive glimmers of light.

"Where are we ? " she asked.

" Far away from everywhere, I should think," he replied eagerly. " Where would you like me to put you down ? "

She asked him to stop at a station, and he did not attempt to disguise his anxiety to leave her.

" I must go to the Chambre," he said. " I do not know what they have been doing to-day."

"Ah, they were sitting to-day ? "

" Yes," he replied, " but there was nothing of importance, I believe—an increase of tariff. But one never knows. I had better just look in."

They took leave of one another easily and amicably. As Madame Worms-Clavelin stepped into a fiacre in the Boulevard de Courcelles, near the fortifications, she heard the newsboys crying the evening papers, and holding them out to the passers-by as they hurried along. She caught sight of a heading in huge letters—" Fall of the Government."

Madame Worms-Clavelin stood for a moment
looking at the men, and listening to the voices dying
away in the rainy night. She reflected that, if
Loyer were really going to send in his resignation
to the President of the Republic, there would be
in all probability no notice in to-morrow's *Officiel*
of the new appointments in the Church. She
reflected that her husband's decoration would not
be included in the last will and testament of the
Minister of the Interior, and that hence the half-
hour she had spent in the blue-curtained fiacre
was of no avail. She had no regret over what had
happened, but did not like doing things to no
purpose.

" Neuilly," she said to the driver, " Boulevard
Bineau, the Convent of the Dames du Saint-Sang."

And she sat pensive and solitary, while the
cries of the newsvendors filled her ears, and
she tried to convince herself that the news was
true. She would not buy a paper, however,
partly out of mistrust and contempt for all newspaper matter, and partly because she was deter-
mined not to rob herself of so much as a half-
penny. She reflected that if the Ministry really
had fallen, just at the moment when she was
being so prodigal of her favours, it was a striking
example of the irony of things and the spite that
hovers ceaselessly about us, like the very atmosphere

we breathe. She asked herself whether Loyer's
secretary-in-chief had not known the news that
was now being shouted abroad while he waited
for her at the park gates. At this thought she
grew scarlet, as though her chastity had been
outraged and her faith betrayed, for if that were
the case Maurice Cheiral had been making game
of her, and that she could not endure. However,
her sound common sense and wide experience soon
came to her aid, assuring her that it was never
safe to trust the newspapers. She thought of Abbé
Guitrel without a qualm, and congratulated herself
on having contributed in ever so small a degree to
the elevation of the excellent priest to the See of
the Blessed Saint Loup. She arranged a few little
details of her toilet the while, so that she might
present a good appearance in the parlour of the
Dames du Saint-Sang who were charged with the
education of her daughter.

The fog was paler and less dense in the deserted
avenues, and the low, damp streets of Neuilly.
Through the gentle rain, the strong, graceful
outlines of the great bare trees were visible.
Madame Worms-Clavelin caught a glimpse of some
poplars, and they reminded her of the country
which she loved more dearly every day.

She reached the barred doorway crowned with a
stone shield bearing the glove in which Joseph of

Arimathea received the sacred blood of the Saviour,
and rang the bell. At her request, the portress sent
for Mademoiselle de Clavelin, and Madame Worms-
Clavelin entered the bright parlour with its horse-
hair chairs. As she sat there before a picture of
the Virgin extending her blessing-laden hands, the
préfet's wife was filled with a strong, sweet feeling
of religion. She was not wholly a Christian, because
she had never been baptized. But her daughter
had been baptized, and was being brought up in
the Catholic faith. Together with the Republic,
Madame Worms-Clavelin felt strong leanings towards a conventional piety, and with a sincere
uplifting of the heart she saluted the kind, blue-
veiled Virgin, to whom well-to-do ladies like
herself poured out their troubles and necessities.
She thanked Providence for all her blessings, as she
sat before the picture of Mary, with her outstretched
arms, and she thanked the Virgin with a mystical
intensity that the Jewish religion had never been
able to satisfy. She was full of gratitude to God,
who had guided her from the miserable days of
her childhood in Montmartre, when she had run
about the greasy streets of the outer boulevards in
her worn-out shoes, until the present time, when
she mixed in the best society, belonged to the
ruling classes, and had a share in the affairs that
governed the country; and she thanked God that

s

in all her negotiations—for life is difficult, and one often needs the help of others—she had, at any rate, never had to come into contact with any but men of position in the world.

" Good evening, mother ! "

Madame Worms-Clavelin drew her daughter under the lamp and examined her teeth ; that was always her first care. Then she looked at her eyes, to see whether she were anæmic or not, saw that her back was straight and that she did not bite her nails. When satisfied on all these points, she inquired as to her work and her conduct. Her solicitude was full of sound common sense and much experience, and altogether she was an excellent mother.

When at last the bell rang for evening study, and it was time to say good-bye, Madame Worms-Clavelin drew from her pocket a box of chocolates. The box was crushed, broken, dilapidated, and as flat as a pancake.

Mademoiselle de Clavelin took it, saying with a laugh :

" Oh, mother ! It looks as if it had been in the wars ! "

" It is this dreadful weather ! " said Madame Worms-Clavelin, with a shrug of her shoulders.

That evening after dinner at the boarding-house she found on the drawing-room table a well-known evening paper whose information she knew to be well authenticated. On reading it, she learned that the Government had not fallen, and was not even in difficulties. It is true that it had been in the minority at the commencement of the sitting, but that was only on the order of the day, and it had immediately been followed by a majority of 105.

The news delighted her, and as she thought of her husband, she said to herself, " Lucien will be pleased to hear that Guitrel has been made bishop."

CHAPTER XXI

"ASK M. Guitrel to come in," said Loyer.

Seated at his desk, the Minister was hardly visible behind the heaps of paper piled upon it; he was a little spectacled old man, with a grey moustache, watery eyes, and a sniff—a cynical, cantankerous old fellow, but an honest man who, in spite of the power and honour that had fallen to his lot, still had the appearance and manner of a professor of the law. He took off his spectacles and wiped them, for he was curious to see the Abbé, the candidate to the episcopal dignity, who had been backed by so many brilliant society women.

Madame de Gromance, the pretty provincial, had been the first to call upon him at the end of December. She had told him, without beating about the bush, that he must appoint the Abbé Guitrel to the see of Tourcoing. The old Minister, who still loved the perfume that clings to a pretty woman, had kept the little hand of Madame de Gromance for a long time between his, stroking

with his thumb the bare space between the glove
and the sleeve where over the blue veins the skin
is softest. He had not gone further, however,
because he was getting old, and everything was an
effort to him, and also he was afraid of appearing
ridiculous in her eyes, for he still had his share of
vanity. His words alone savoured of impropriety,
and, according to his invariable custom, he inquired
for Madame de Gromance's " old Royalist," as he
familiarly called her husband. His eyes had become
tearful behind their bluish glasses, and his face had
creased itself into a thousand little wrinkles at the
excellence of the jest.

The idea that the " old Royalist " was a wronged
husband filled the Minister of Justice and Public
Worship with what really was inordinate glee. As
he thought of it, he looked at Madame de Gromance
with more curiosity, interest, and pleasure than
was perhaps in the case justifiable, but from the
ruins of his amorous nature he was building a
series of mental amusements, the most intense of
which was to gloat over the misfortune of M. de
Gromance in the very presence of its voluptuous
cause.

During the six months in which he had been
Minister of the Interior in a former Radical
Cabinet, he had received from Worms-Clavelin
private and confidential notes, telling him all about

the Gromance ménage, so that he knew all there
was to know about Clotilde's lovers, and delighted
in the knowledge that they were numerous. He
had received the beautiful petitioner with every
kindness, promising to look into M. Guitrel's case,
but committing himself no further, for he was a
good Republican, and did not believe in subor-
dinating affairs of state to a woman's caprice.

Then, too, the Baronne de Bonmont, who was
reputed to have the most beautiful shoulders in
Paris, had spoken in favour of Abbé Guitrel at the
Élysée soirées. Finally, Madame Worms-Clavelin,
the *préfet's* wife, a very charming woman, had
whispered a word in his ear concerning the good
Abbé.

Loyer was very curious to see the priest who had
fluttered so many feminine hearts. He wondered
whether he was about to behold one of the great
sturdy becassocked fellows that of latter days the
Church has thrown into public gatherings, sending
them as far even as the Chamber of Deputies, one
of those young, full-blooded, outspoken clerical
tribunes of the people—headstrong and shrewd,
with a power over simple men and women.

The Abbé Guitrel entered the study, his head
upon one side, and holding his hat before him in
his clasped hands. He was not unprepossessing,
but his desire to please, and his respect for the

powers that be, made his habitual carefully assumed
priestly dignity less apparent than usual.

Loyer noticed his three chins and domed head,
his portly form, his narrow shoulders, and his
unctuousness. He was quite an old man too.

"What do the women want with him ? "
he thought.

The interview was trifling on either side; but,
after questioning M. Guitrel on some points of
ecclesiastical administration, Loyer gathered from
the fat man's replies that his views were both
sensible and fair.

He remembered that the Director of Public
Worship, M. Mostart, was not against the nomination of Abbé Guitrel to the See of Tourcoing.
Truth to tell, M. Mostart had not given him much
information on the subject. Since there had
been such a rapid succession of clerical and anti-
clerical cabinets, the Director of Public Worship
had not dabbled overmuch in the making of
bishops ; the matter had become too delicate
of handling. He had a house at Joinville, and was
fond of gardening and fishing. His dearest dream
was to write a chatty history of the Bobino Theatre,
which he had known in its palmy days. He was
growing old, was a prudent man, and did not stick
obstinately to his own opinion. The evening
before he had said to Loyer, " I propose Abbé

Guitrel, but there's nothing to choose between Abbé Guitrel and Abbé Lantaigne, it's six of one and half a dozen of the other!" Those were the very words of the Director of Public Worship, but Loyer was himself an old doctor at law, and always able to make nice distinctions.

M. Guitrel seemed to him sensible enough, and not too fanatical.

"You are not ignorant of the fact, Monsieur l'Abbé," he said, "that the late Bishop of Tourcoing, M. Duclou, tended to become intolerant in the latter part of his life, and gave an unreasonable amount of work to the Council of State. What is your opinion on the subject?"

"Alas," replied the Abbé Guitrel, with a sigh, "it is quite true that in his declining years, as he neared the period of eternal blessedness, Monseigneur Duclou made some rather unfortunate declarations. The situation was a difficult one then, but things have greatly altered, and his successor will be able to labour quietly towards the establishment of peace. What he will have to aim at is real peace. The road to it is marked; he will have to enter upon it resolutely and follow it to the end. As a matter of fact, laws dealing with education and the Army do not give rise nowadays to any difficulties, and all that really remains is the question of the taxation of religious communities.   This question, we must allow, is peculiarly important in a diocese like Tourcoing, which, if I may say so, is plastered with all kinds of religious institutions.   I have studied it at length, and, if you wish, can speak of the conclusions to which this study has led me."

" The clergy," said Loyer, " dislike parting with their money.   That is the truth."

" Nobody likes it, Monsieur le Ministre," returned Abbé Guitrel, " and Your Excellency, such an adept in all that relates to finance, must realize that there is a way of shearing the ratepayer without making him complain.   Why not use the same method with our poor monks, who are too good Frenchmen not to be good ratepayers ?   You must bear in mind, Monsieur le Ministre, that they are subject in the first case to the ordinary taxes that everybody pays."

" Naturally," put in Loyer.

" Secondly, to taxes on inalienable property."

" And do you complain of that ? " inquired the Minister.

" Not at all," replied the Abbé.   " I am merely enumerating them all—quick reckonings make long friends.   Thirdly, to a tax of four per cent on the income accruing from lands, houses, furniture, and money ;   and, fourthly, they are liable to the increment duty, as established by the laws of the

28th of December, 1880, and the 29th of December, 1884. It is only the principle underlying this last tax, as you know, Monsieur le Ministre, that has been contested by several communities. The agitation has not yet died down everywhere, and it is on this point, Monsieur le Ministre, that I take the liberty of expressing the views which would actuate me, were I to have the honour of occupying the see of the Blessed Saint Loup."

As a sign of attention, the Minister turned round in his chair, and faced the Abbé, who went on in the following terms :

" As a matter of principle, Monsieur le Ministre, I disapprove of the spirit of revolt, and dislike any tumultuous or systematic claiming of rights, and in this I only comply with the Encyclical beginning ' *Diuturnum illud*,' in which Leo XIII, following the example of St. Paul, exhorts his people to obedience towards the civil authorities. So much for principle ; let us now look fact in the face. As a matter of fact, I find that the religious in the diocese of Tourcoing are placed in such different positions with regard to rates and taxes that universality of action is thereby rendered exceedingly difficult. In this diocese there are authorized and unauthorized communities, some communities dedicated to works of charity among the poor, the aged, and the orphan, and some whose sole aim and object is a life of spiritual contemplation. They are taxed differently, according to their different purposes. It is my opinion that the very opposition of their interests breaks down resistance, unless their bishop himself directs the tenor of their claims, a thing which, for my part, I should avoid, if I were their spiritual head. I would willingly see uncertainty and division among the communities of my diocese if by so doing I could ensure the peace of the Church as a whole. As far as my secular clergy were concerned," added the priest in a firm voice, " I would answer for them as a general answers for his troops."

Having thus spoken, M. Guitrel apologized for having given such free vent to his thoughts, and wasted the precious time of His Excellency.

Old Loyer made no answer, but he nodded approval. For a parson, Guitrel was not so difficult to get on with after all, he thought.

CHAPTER XXII

ADAME DE BONMONT dismissed her carriage, and, hailing a cab, drove to the street where, amid the rumble of drays and the whistle of engines, she carried on her love affair. She would have preferred to see her Rara in a region adorned with gardens, but love is sometimes shy under the myrtles or by the murmuring fountains. Madame de Bonmont's thoughts were sad as she drove along the streets where the lamps were just beginning to glimmer through the misty evening light. Guitrel had indeed been appointed Bishop of Tourcoing, and she rejoiced thereat, but joy did not possess her soul completely. Rara, with his black humour and ferocious desires, worried her terribly. Now she went in fear and trembling to the rendezvous, to which in former times she had so eagerly looked forward. Confiding and retiring by nature, she dreaded, on his account as well as her own, anything in the nature of danger, catastrophe, or scandal. Her lover's mental

278

attitude, which had never been satisfactory, had quite suddenly grown worse. Since the suicide of Colonel Henry he had become dreadful to look upon. The bitterness in his blood had acted like vitriol upon his countenance, as it were searing his forehead, his eyelids, his cheeks, with marks of fire and brimstone. For the last fortnight mysterious causes had kept her dear one absent from the flat which he rented opposite the Moulin-Rouge, and which was his legal domicile. He had his letters forwarded to him, and received visitors in the little suite which Madame de Bonmont had taken for quite a different use.

Slowly and sadly she went up the stairs, but even on the very threshold of the door the hope of finding the delightful Rara of former days stirred her heart. Alas, her hope was vain, she was greeted with bitter words :

" What do you come here for ? You despise me like all the rest."

She protested at such cruelty.

She did not despise him—on the contrary, her loving animal nature led her to admire him. She put her painted, yet youthful, lips to her lover's mouth, and kissed him sobbingly ; but, pushing her away, he began to pace furiously up and down the two blue-tapestried rooms.

Noiselessly she untied the little parcel of cakes

she had brought with her, and said in a hopeless, toneless voice:

" Will you have a *baba*? It is kirsch, just as you like them," and she handed him the cake between two dainty sugary fingers. But he refused to see or hear her, and continued his fierce, monotonous promenade.

Then, with tear-dimmed eyes and bosom that heaved with sighs, she lifted the thick black veil which, mask-like, covered the upper part of her face, and silently commenced to eat a chocolate *éclair*.

At last, however, not knowing what to do or to say, she took a jewel-case from her pocket, and, opening it, displayed for Rara the bishop's ring which it contained, saying in a timid voice:

" Look at M. Guitrel's ring. It is a pretty stone, isn't it? It is an Hungarian amethyst. Do you think M. Guitrel will like it? "

" I don't care a damn! "

She put the case down on the toilet table in despair, while he, resuming the usual current of his thoughts, growled out:

" There's no mistake about it! I will do for one of them! "

She looked at him doubtfully, for she had noticed that he was always threatening to kill everybody, and that he killed no one. He divined her hidden thought. It was dreadful.

" I knew that you despised me too," he said.

He nearly struck her, and she wept bitterly ; eventually he calmed down, however, and drew her a terrible picture of his financial embarrassments.

She wept at the picture, but did not promise to give him much, because it was against her principles to give money to a lover, and, besides, she feared he might go away altogether if he had the means to do so.

When she left the little blue rooms she was so upset that she quite forgot the amethyst ring lying on the toilet table.

CHAPTER XXIII

"ARE you working, dear Master, do I disturb you?" asked M. Goubin, entering M. Bergeret's study.

"Not at all," replied the professor. "I was amusing myself by translating a Greek text of the Alexandrine period, discovered in a tomb at Philæ."

"I should be very glad if you would read me your translation, dear Master," said M. Goubin.

"With pleasure," replied M. Bergeret, and he began:

CONCERNING HERCULES ATIMOS.

Deeds are commonly ascribed to the one and only Hercules which in reality have been accomplished by other heroes bearing the same name. That which Orpheus teaches us concerning the Thracian Hercules relates to the god rather than to the hero. I will not dwell upon this. The Tyrians tell of another Hercules to whom they attribute labours so prodigious that they are difficult to accept. What is less known is that

Alcmena gave birth to twins who were exactly alike, and who each received the name of Hercules. The one was the son of Jupiter and the other of Amphitryon. On account of his great deeds, the former attained the right to drink from the cup of Hebe at the table of the gods, and we look upon him as a god. The second was unworthy, that is why he was called Hercules Atimos.

What I know of him I have learned from an inhabitant of Eleusis, a wise and prudent man who has collected together many ancient legends. This is what he told me:

Hercules Atimos, the son of Amphitryon, when nearing manhood, received from his father a bow and arrows, forged by Vulcan, which dealt certain death to any creature whom they struck.

Now one day, when shooting wild cranes on the slopes of Cithæron, he met a herdsman who addressed him thus:

" Son of Amphitryon, there is an evil man who daily steals some of our cattle. Thou art full of youth and vigour. If thou canst find the thief and strike him with one of thy magic arrows, thou wilt gain great praise. But he is not easy of approach, for his feet are larger than the feet of other men, and he is very fleet."

Atimos promised the herdsman that he would punish the brigand, and went upon his way. Hiding

T

in the mountain gorges, he saw at a distance the
figure of a man who appeared to him evil. Thinking
it was the cattle-stealer, he killed him with his
arrows. But while the man's blood was still fresh
upon the wild anemones, Pallas Athene, the bright-
eyed goddess, descended from Olympus, and came
to meet Atimos, who did not recognize her, for she
was disguised as an old servant of King Amphitryon.
And the goddess spoke to him thus:

" Divine son of Amphitryon, the man thou hast
killed was not a stealer of cattle, but a good man.
The guilty man is easily recognized by the print of
his feet in the dust, for they are larger than those
of other men. The dead man's conduct was
irreproachable, and his life a life of innocence.
Therefore shalt thou pray with tears to the divine
Apollo to restore him to life. Apollo will not
refuse thy request if thou pleadest with outstretched
supplicating hands."

Full of anger, however, Atimos replied:

" I have punished this man for his wickedness.
Dost thou think, old man, that I know not what I
do and strike at random? Peace! Get thee gone,
thou madman, or thou shalt repent thy audacity."

Some young shepherds who were gambolling
with their goats upon the slopes of Cithæron
hearing the words of Atimos, received them with
such shouts of praise that the mountain resounded

and the ancient pine trees stirred and quivered. And Pallas Athene, the bright-eyed goddess, returned to snowy Olympus.

Atimos, however, had resumed his journey, and soon found himself upon the tracks of the cattle-thief, whom he could see at a little distance ahead. He recognized him quite easily by his footprints in the sand, for they were much greater than those of other men.

Then thought the hero to himself, " It is necessary that men believe in the innocence of this man, so that they may believe I have slain the guilty one, and that my glory be made known among men."

With this thought in his mind, he called the man and said to him: " Friend, I honour thee because thou art good and thy thoughts just." Then, drawing from his quiver one of the arrows made by Vulcan, he gave it to the man with these words, " Take this arrow made by Vulcan. All those who see thee with it will honour thee, and thou wilt be judged worthy of the friendship of a hero."

Thus spoke he. The thief took the arrow and went away. And divine Athene, the bright-eyed goddess, descended from snowy Olympus. She disguised herself as a gentle shepherd, and, coming up to Atimos, said: " Son of Amphitryon, in absolving the guilty man thou hast killed the innocent a second time. And this action shall not bring thee glory among men."

But Atimos did not recognize the goddess, and believing her to be a shepherd, he cried in fury: "Chicken-heart, vain babbler, dog, I will tear out thy soul!" And he lifted against Pallas Athene his bow, the wood of which was harder than the iron of the arrows forged by Vulcan.

"The rest is missing," said M. Bergeret, replacing the papers upon his table.

"What a pity!" said M. Goubin.

"It is a pity," said M. Bergeret. "I have been much interested in translating this Greek text; one must have a change sometimes from everyday affairs."

CHAPTER XXIV

S evening fell, Madame de Bonmont with anxious heart hailed a cab and drove to Rara's rooms, for she wished to see him again and to recover the amethyst ring. But she feared some disaster. When the cab crossed the Pont de l'Europe and stopped in front of her lover's door she saw that the road was black with hats and coats. Something was going on that reminded her of a funeral or a removal. Men were heaping portfolios and piles of papers into a cab, others were bringing along a little box which Madame de Bonmont recognised as the old military trunk filled with stamped papers in which Rara had so often plunged his flushed arms and his furious, hairy visage.

As she stood there, frozen with terror, she heard the voice of the dishevelled *concierge* whisper in her ear:

" Don't come in. Be off as fast as you can ! The police are here with the magistrate and the commissioner. They have seized your gentleman's papers and sealed up everything."

The cab carried away a prostrate Madame de Bonmont. In the depths of despair at her lost love she was, however, conscious of this thought:

"And Monseigneur Guitrel's ring, which has been sealed with the rest!"

CHAPTER XXV

EOPLE had been talking about it for three months. M. Bergeret learned that he had friends in Paris who had never seen him, and friends such as these are the surest; their actions are governed by sensible, masterly, positive reasons, and, if only their report is favourable, they are sure of a hearing. M. Bergeret's friends thought that his place was in Paris, and suggested bringing him there. M. Leterrier did all he could to bring this about, and at last it was arranged.

M. Bergeret was appointed Professor at the Sorbonne. As he left the house of M. le Doyen Torquet, who had apprised him in the most formal terms of his nomination, M. Bergeret, finding himself in the street again, looked at the slate roofs, the familiar free-stone walls, the shaving basin that swung gently to and fro over the door of the hairdresser, the sign of the red cow over the milkman's, and the little bronze Triton, with water streaming from his mouth, at the corner of the Faubourg de

Josde; and all these familiar things appeared suddenly strange in his eyes. His feet had suddenly become unacquainted with the pavements on which he had so long and so often gone his way, with feet rendered heavy by sadness or fatigue, or made light by some slight happiness or amusement. The town, with its towers and steeples standing up against the grey sky, looked to him like some strange, far-away dream city, rather the picture of a city than the reality. And the picture grew smaller and smaller. People, as well as things, seemed far-away and diminished in his eyes. The postman, two women, and the clerk of the court whom he met, looked, to him, like people on a cinematograph screen, absolutely unreal and belonging to quite another world than his.

After a few minutes of this strange feeling, he pulled himself up, for he was both thoughtful and quick to read his own motives, thus providing himself with an inexhaustible subject for surprise, sarcasm, and pity.

"Come now," he said to himself, "here is a town in which I have lived for fifteen years, and which suddenly becomes strange to me because I am about to leave it. More than that, it has, to a certain extent, already become unreal to me. Now that it is no longer my own town, it ceases to exist, and is nothing but a vain image. The reason is that the many interesting things it contains were only interesting in so far as they directly affected me. As soon as they cease to do that, they practically do not exist as far as I am concerned. And thus, this populous city, situated on the hills that border a great river, this ancient Gaulish town, this colony where the Romans built temples and a circus ; this strong city that went through three memorable sieges, where two councils were held, which was enriched with a basilica, the crypt of which is still in existence, a cathedral, a college, sixteen parish churches, plus sixty chapels, a town hall, markets, hospitals, and palaces ; this town which in very ancient times formed a part of the royal domain, became the capital of a vast province, and still bears on the fronton of the governor's palace, now turned into barracks, the civic coat of arms surrounded by lions and the Virtues ; this town which to-day contains an archbishop's palace, a Faculty of Letters, a Faculty of Science, a Court of Appeal, and a Court of Justice ; the chief town of a rich department only existed in reference to myself. It was peopled by myself alone ; I was the only cause of its existence. It is high time for me to go ; the town is fading away. I never knew that my mind was subjective to such a mad extent. A man never knows himself, and is a monster without realizing it."

Thus did M. Bergeret examine himself with praiseworthy sincerity. As he was passing the church of Saint-Exupère, however, he stopped under the porch of the Last Judgment. He had always loved the old legendary sculptures, and taken an interest in the stories graven upon the stone. One devil in particular, who had a dog's head on his shoulders, and a man's face on the nether portion of his anatomy, had a peculiar fascination for him. He was occupied in dragging a long file of damned souls chained together, and his two countenances expressed absolute contentment. There was also a little monk whom an angel was trying to draw up by his hands, while a devil dragged him down by the feet. M. Bergeret loved that one, but he had never before looked with so much interest at these objects which he was now on the point of leaving.

He could not take his eyes away from them. The naïve idea of the universe expressed in stone by men who had been dead for more than five hundred years touched him, and seemed to him lovable in its absurdity. He regretted never having studied it more closely or examined it more sympathetically. He remembered that this porch of the Last Judgment which he had seen gilded by the rays of the sun and whitened by the moonbeams, in the joyous summer time and the dark winter days, would be with him only a little longer, and then he would see it no more.

He realized then that he was attached to things by invisible links not to be broken asunder without pain, and his heart was suddenly filled with great veneration for his town. He loved her old walls and her old trees. He went out of his way to go up the Mall and look at a favourite elm that grew there, the one he always sat beneath at the close of the long summer days. The beautiful tree was now bare of foliage, and its strong, slender framework stood out naked and black against the sky. M. Bergeret gazed at it long. The tranquil giant was motionless and silent, and the mystery of its peaceful life gave rise to deep meditation on the part of the man who was about to enter upon a new phase of his destiny.

It was thus M. Bergeret learned that he loved his mother soil and the town where he had suffered tribulation and tasted quiet happiness.

CHAPTER XXVI

ONSEIGNEUR GUITREL, Bishop of Tourcoing, addressed to the President of the Republic the following letter, the text of which was published *in extenso* by the *Semaine religieuse*, the *Vérité*, the *Étendard*, the *Études sérieuses*, and several other diocesan papers:

" MONSIEUR LE PRÉSIDENT,

"Before bringing to your notice several just causes for complaint and divers claims which are only too well founded, allow me for one short instant to enjoy the keen delight of feeling that I am in perfect accord with you on a point which must affect us both; allow me, realizing as I do the feelings that must have swayed you during these long days of trial and of consolation, to join with you in an outburst of patriotic gratitude. Oh, how your generous soul must have suffered when you saw that handful of misguided men cast insult at the Army under the pretext of defending justice and truth, as though justice and truth could exist in opposition

294

to social order and the hierarchy of power established by God Himself upon this earth! And
how that heart of yours must have rejoiced at
the sight of the whole nation, without exception
of party, rising as one man to acclaim our brave
Army, the Army of Clovis, Charlemagne, and
St. Louis, of Godefroy de Bouillon, Jeanne d'Arc
and Bayard; to embrace her cause and avenge her
wrongs. Oh, with what satisfaction must you have
witnessed the watchful wisdom of the nation as it
frustrated the devices of the proud and the evil-doer!

"Certainly one cannot deny that the honour of
such praiseworthy conduct is due to France as a
whole. But you are too clear-sighted, M. le
Président, not to have recognized the Church and
her faithful members in the van of the supporters
of law and authority. They were in the front
rank of the battle, saluting with confidence and
respect the Army and her chiefs. And was it not
the right place for the servants of Him Who has
called Himself the God of Armies, and Who, to
use the words of Bossuet, has sanctified them in
calling Himself by that name? Thus you will
always find in us the surest upholders of law and
order, and the obedience which we have not refused
even to princes that persecuted us will never tire. ·
In return for this may your Government ever look
peacefully upon us, and so make our obedience a

joy! Our hearts must exult at sight of the warlike
array which makes us feared by other nations, and
at sight of you yourself in your place of honour,
surrounded by your brilliant staff, like King Saul,
that great and courageous man who always attached
the bravest warriors to his person. *Nam quem-
cumque viderat Saul virum fortem et aptum ad
prælium, sociabat eum sibi* (1 Kings xiv. 52).

" Oh, would that I could end this letter as I have
commenced it, with words of joy and gladness, and
how happy should I be, M. le Président, if I could
associate your venerated name with the declaration
of peace in the Church as I have associated it with
the victories gained before our eyes by the spirit
of authority over the spirit of discord. But, alas,
it cannot be! I must bring to your notice a subject
of great sorrow; must afflict your soul by the
spectacle of a great grief. I shall accomplish
an irresistible duty in bringing your mind to bear
upon an open and bleeding wound which must be
healed. It is to my interest to tell you certain
painful truths, and to your interest to listen. My
pastoral duty compels me to speak. Placed by the
grace of the Sovereign Pontiff upon the See of the
Blessèd Saint Loup, successor as I am of so many
holy apostles and vigilant pastors, should I be the
legitimate heir of their devoted labours if I had
not the courage to continue them? *Alii labora-*

verunt, et vos in labores eorum introistis (Ecc. viii. 9).
It is therefore fitting that my feeble voice should
uplift itself until it reach your ears.   It is also fitting
that you lend an attentive ear to my words, for the
subject I am about to discuss is worthy the thought
of a ruler.   *Princeps vero ea, quæ digna sunt principe,
cogitabit* (Is. xxxii.).

"But how can I broach the subject without
immediately feeling myself overcome by over-
whelming grief ?   How can I, without weeping,
point out to you the state of the religious whose
spiritual head I am ?   For it is of them I would
speak, M. le Président.   As I entered my diocese,
how heart-rending were the sights that met my gaze
on all sides.   In the sacred buildings consecrated to
the education of children, the cure of the sick, and
the care of the aged, the instruction of our priests
and the contemplation of the divine mysteries, I
found nothing but anxious faces and sad looks.
There, where the joy of innocence and the quietude
of labour formerly reigned, a dark anxiety has
settled.   Sighs go up to heaven, and from all lips
the same cry of anguish, 'Who will care for our
sick and aged ?   What will become of our little
children ?   Where shall we retire to pray ? '   These
were the words that greeted the shepherd of the
diocese of Tourcoing, such were the words of the
monks and nuns who knelt at his feet and kissed

his hands, for they have been robbed of that which is theirs by right, of that which is also the right of our poor, our widows and orphans, the bread of our clergy, and the viaticum of our missionaries. Thus, at the moment of total ruin, our monks and nuns bewailed their fate while they waited for the tax-collectors to outrage the sanctuary of our cloistered virgins, and even to seize the sacred vessels on the altar.

" This, then, is the state to which our religious communities are reduced by the enforcement of the different taxation laws to which I have referred, if such mad and criminal enactments can be called laws.· If you will but examine the position in which our religious orders are placed by these spoliative measures, dignified by the name of laws, the expressions of which I make use will not appear to you excessive, and a moment's attention on your part will make you share my feelings. Having regard to the fact that religious bodies are subject to the general taxation, it is iniquitous to force further taxes upon them ; that will at once strike you as an injustice, and I can point out others equally unjust. But as regards this thing in particular, M. le Président, allow me to protest both firmly and respectfully. I have not sufficient authority to speak in the name of the entire Church, but I am sure that I do not stray from the right path when I declare as an

essential principle of justice that the State has no
right to impose burdens upon the Church. The
Church pays what is demanded of her, she pays as
an act of grace, but she is under no obligation to do
so. Her ancient exemption from taxation proceeded
from her sovereignty, for the sovereign pays no
tribute. She can always enter a claim to those ancient
rights when and where it suits her convenience ;
she can no more renounce her just claims than she
can renounce her duties and sovereign privileges,
and, as matters are, she gives proof of the most
admirable powers of renunciation. That is all.
Having stated my objections, I will now proceed
with my evidence.

" The religious bodies are subject to the following
duties :

" Firstly, general taxation, as I have just stated.

" Secondly, taxes on inalienable property.

" Thirdly, a tax of four per cent on income (Acts
of 1880 and 1884).

" Fourthly, liability under the ' droit d'accroisse-
ment,' the monstrous effects of which are supposed
to have been modified by what is called the ' droit
d'abonnement,' by which the Government annually
deducts from the estimated portion of deceased
members the sum of eleven francs twenty-five per
cent, including the decimes. It is true that, by a
mock kindness which is in reality merely a refine-

U

ment of perfidy and injustice, the law allows the charitable and educational institutions to be relieved of this charge, on account of their utility, as though the houses where our holy women pray God to pardon the crimes of France and to enlighten her blinded rulers were not as useful, more useful even, than schools and hospitals !

" But it was necessary to disunite the common interests, and in order to do so differential treatment had to be meted out. The idea was to disintegrate and paralyse resistance ; this again was the idea that actuated the Government when they fixed the tax of 30 per cent for recognized religious institutions, and at 40 per cent for the unrecognized, payable annually, on the value of property both real and personal, so that the latter, who are not permitted to hold property, are judged liable to pay, and to pay even more than the others.

" To sum up, for the further burden of our religious bodies to the common taxes are added the tax on inalienable property, the income tax of 4 per cent, and the so-called increment duties, which are not modified but accentuated by what is called the ' droit d'abonnement ' or subscription duty. Is this endurable ? Is it possible to find in the whole world another such abominable example of spoliation ? No, you must admit, M. le Président, that it is not.

" And when the religious orders of my diocese

asked me what they were to do, could I give them any other reply than the following: 'Resist the law! It is your right and duty to oppose injustice! Resist the law! Say to them, "We cannot do it. *Non possumus.*"'

"They are resolved so to do, M. le Président, and all our religious bodies, recognized or un-recognized, teaching, charitable or cloistered, des-tined to foreign missions or to lives of monastic retreat, are agreed, in spite of the inequality with which they are assessed, upon a stubborn resistance. They have realized that the different forms of treatment meted out to them by your so-called laws are uniformly iniquitous, and that it behoves them to join together in a common defence. Their resolve is unshakable. After having paved the way to it, I support their resolution, and in so doing feel assured that I am not failing in the obedience I owe to authority and to the law, and which I whole-heartedly render to you both as a matter of conscience and religion. I feel sure that I am not misjudging your power, which can only be exercised for the maintenance of justice. *Ecce in justitia regnabit rex* (Paralip. xxii. 22).

"In his pastoral letter *Diuturnum illud* His Holi-ness Leo XIII has expressly declared that the faith-ful may dispense with obedience to civil power if the latter issue orders that openly disregard natural and divine rights. ' If a man,' he has said in this admirable letter, ' finds himself forced to infringe either the law of God or the law of man, he should follow the precepts of Jesus Christ, and reply like the apostles, " It is better to obey God than man." To act thus is not to merit the reproach of disobedience, for as soon as the will of a ruler is in opposition to the will and law of God he exceeds his power, justice is corrupted, and henceforth his authority is impotent because, in so far as it is unjust, it ceases to exist.'

"Believe me it is not without deep and protracted meditation that I have encouraged the religious bodies under my control to make the necessary resistance. I have weighed the temporal loss that may, perhaps, result, and such consideration has not stopped me. When we reply to your tax-gatherers, ' *Non possumus,*' you will attempt to overcome our resistance by force. But how will you achieve your end ? Will you lay hands upon our recognized bodies ? Dare you ? Upon our non-recognized bodies ? Can you ? Will you show a pitiful courage and sell our goods and the objects dedicated to divine worship? And if it is indeed true that neither the poverty of the former nor the sacred nature of the latter will preserve them from your rapacity, you must learn, and the wives and children of those who aid and abet you must learn, that those who enter upon such a course run the risk of excommunication, the terrible effects of which strike fear into even the most hardened sinners. And all those who consent to buy anything proceeding from any such unlawful sale expose themselves to the same penalty.

" And if we are robbed of our belongings, hunted from our dwellings, the injury will not be to us, but to you, who will be covered with the shame of un-precedented scandal. You can retaliate most cruelly upon us, but no threat can frighten us ; we fear neither prison nor chains. The manacled hands of priests and confessors have delivered the Church ere now. Come what may, we shall pay nothing, we may not, we cannot. *Non possumus*.

" Before arriving at such an extremity I thought it only right, M. le Président, to place the matter before you, in the hope that you would inquire into it with the whole-hearted firmness God bestows upon the rulers who place their trust in Him. May you, with His help, find a remedy for the crying evils I have placed before you. God grant, M. le Président, God grant that, when you have examined the injustice of the taxation as regards our religious bodies, you may be guided less by your counsellors than by your own sense of justice. For, if the chief may take counsel of others, it is his own

counsel he should follow.   As Solomon has said,
' Counsel in the heart of a man is like unto deep
water.'   *Sicut aqua profunda, sic consilium in corde
viri* (Prov. xx. 5).

" With the deepest respect, etc., I have the
honour, M. le Président, to be

> " Your obedient servant,
> " JOACHIM,
> " Bishop of Tourcoing."

The letter of the Bishop of Tourcoing was pub-
lished on January 14th.

On the 30th of the same month the *Agence
Hava* sent the following communication to the
papers :

" The cabinet met yesterday at the Élysée. It
was decided at the meeting that the Minister of
Public Worship should apply to the Council d'État
for a writ against Monseigneur Guitrel, Bishop of
Tourcoing, in connexion with a letter addressed by
him to the President of the Republic."

www.ingramcontent.com/pod-product-compliance
Lightning Source LLC
Chambersburg PA
CBHW030342020726
47493CB00003B/647